Then There Was Two

Ai Bei

Translated by Howard Goldblatt

MarkoPolski Books
San Francisco • Warsaw

ISBN: 0-615-69455-1

ISBN-13: 978-0615694559

CONTENTS

TRANSLATOR'S NOTE

During the course of translation it became apparent that some of the descriptions of American life and institutions, and the role of Chinese immigrants and visitors in them, did not necessarily square with reality. At first these inconsistencies were changed, but following consultations with the author, the original text was restored owing to our shared belief in the importance of revealing misunderstandings and misperceptions of the West prevalent among people in China, including artists and intellectuals. Minor factual errors have been corrected.

AUTHOR'S NOTE

I came to the USA in 1989 as a participant in a program by the United States Information Agency for foreign writers and journalists. During the visa interview on 7th of October 1988, a member of the embassy staff asked me if I could write a short story or a novel about Chinese students in the United States. I promised I would. The second novella in this volume is the result of that promise.

Then There Was Two

Chapter 1

Two always had a far-off look in his eyes, especially around Chinese. During his three years and four months in the States, he'd already held a dozen or so jobs and moved at least five times. He got along fine when talking with redheads and blondes, but as soon as he was around someone with black hair and eyes he just clammed up.

Two sometimes let his hair grow down to his shoulders and sometimes wore it so short you'd think a dog had gnawed on his head, and he looked like one of those punks. He was too lazy to worry about it.

Two always wore stonewashed jeans — summer, spring, winter, and fall. He wasn't following a fad, just lazy.

Two was blessed with the almond-shaped 'phoenix" eyes of a bewitching maiden and dainty hands that were in stark contrast to the rippling muscles on his chest and arms. He looked like a woman with a man's chest or a man with a woman's hands and eyes.

Two walked with such utter concentration he was always bumping into trees, or walls, or pedestrians. Fortunately for him, Americans don't normally butt into other people's business, not even their own parents', so except for his fellow countrymen, who loved to discuss Two's physical disability, no one, not his landlady nor anybody at school, ever commented on his eccentric behavior.

At 10:30 Two jumped out of bed, took a quick cold shower, ran a toothbrush over his teeth a couple of times, flipped through some supermarket ads, started up his beat-up old jalopy — a pickup truck — and drove into the parking lot of Smith's Supermarket.

"Sample these cocktail sausages, 25 percent off, nine for ninety nine cents..." An enormous, gray-haired, blue-eyed woman was trying to entice shoppers with a tray full of cocktail sausages on toothpicks.

Two walked up, picked out two of the longest, fattest sausages on the tray, and popped them into his mouth. He was still chewing them as he ran off to a toaster-oven display: "Pizza samples"

"Sample these caviar crackers."

"Sample some of this banana bread."

"…"

After several trips, Two wiped his greasy mouth and sauntered over to the fruit stand, where he sampled all the grapes — green, purple, oval, round — then picked up a snow pear with two dainty fingers, slipped it between his teeth, and savored it slowly. Strolling over to the barrels filled with nuts and candies, he sampled his favorites and a few he'd never seen before. Then, carefree as could be, he walked up to the exit — *whoosh* — the automatic doors slid open, allowing him to walk regally out of the supermarket.

At the library, Two spent half an hour flipping through the latest newspapers and magazines, then sat down at a computer terminal and logged on to the news net, where he was momentarily caught up in stories about a flood in Africa and the plight of the Vietnamese boat people in Hong Kong. He then chose a comfy-looking sofa and lay down to enjoy the sight of all the human limbs among the forest of table legs spread out before him: legs stretching and legs curling under, feet liberated from their shoes and stepping on the other; knees together, legs spread open, male, female… He could tell the nationality, personality, and study habits just by looking at the legs and feet. He often ogled like this until his eyes got sore.

Two rushed into the classroom, barely a step ahead of Professor Henry. He looked around at pair after pair of wide-eyed faces, white pages of opened textbooks and notebooks… His thin,

5

arching brows jumped slightly, his bewitching 'phoenix' eyes grew lackluster, and he sat down like a robot, without moving.

Professor Henry drew a long arc on the board, gripping the chalk so tightly that neither roaring flames nor a prying knife could have dislodged it. He added a flurry of dots with a fistful of chalk, which he then tossed into the wastebasket behind him as he walked out of the classroom to wash his hands.

The bewildered students wandered if maybe the art professor had stumbled into the wrong room or the political-science professor had a fever.

Professor Henry walked back into the classroom drying his hands. Lecture number one, he said in an even, leisurely tone. How to become a bad person. "What's a politician? Dirty hands!" he answered his own question theatrically.

"Brilliant! A politician is dirty hands!" Two shouted in Chinese, clapping his dainty hands excitedly. His classmates echoed his delight, nearly turning the classroom into a circus. Unable to contain his wild joy, Two shook his desk until it creaked, drawing the stares of students around him. A minute later, when their attention was elsewhere, he slipped out the back door and ran spiritedly through the stand of pines and the flower bed, smacking branches and trampling carnations in the snow on his way to the indoor pool for a relaxing swim. As he floated on his back he gazed up through the glass ceiling at a cloud in the sky, trying to focus his thoughts. When his stomach began to growl, he quickly got dressed and ran over to the student store, where he dug through the seven or eight pockets in his clothes, coming up with a measly two coins. He walked around the sales counter twice, but couldn't find a single snack for less than fifty cents. So he strode out of the student store and stood in front of a soft-drink dispensing machine in the corridor, cautiously choosing a can of tomato juice. He took a big swig.

6

Zhu Li came walking up to him, the outline of her hard nipples visible through her pinafore, which was so popular among high-school girls. She was smiling broadly.

Pretending he was looking for something, Two tried to make himself scarce by running into the student store.

"Hey, what are you hiding from? You think I'm a tiger or something? You don't have to be afraid of me."

Suddenly tongue-tied, Two held up the can of tomato juice and said it was delicious.

"I don't care if it's delicious or not. Take me to a party, okay? Hm? Hm?"

Seeing her act like a spoiled little girl, Two retreated a few steps and said he couldn't go.

"You're afraid of your own shadow!"

Two snickered, picked up his schoolbag, and started to walk off.

Zhu Li reached out and stopped him, brushing one of her breasts against him, maybe intentionally. "I won't let you go. His wife will get jealous if I don't bring a date. Some things are more trouble than they're worth. Help me out, okay? Dear Two, dear sweet Two."

Two's stomach was growling, and it was time to get moving.

But Zhu Li was right behind him, acting spoiled and scolding him gently. "Good old Two, there'll be lots of food, and you can watch his new movie. So what's wrong? If I take someone like you, I don't think he or his wife will get jealous."

Two didn't catch most of what she said, but the words "lots of food" got his juices flowing. He spun around. "What time?"

The overjoyed Zhu Li put her arm in his. "Right now."

Two spotted a banana sticking out of Zhu Li's backpack and reached out to take it. She slapped his wrist. "Good old Two, wait till we get there. There'll be more than we can handle."

Two took the banana anyway, peeled and ate it as he shuffled along listlessly behind Zhu Li, turning one corner after another until they walked into a small building that glistened more brightly than the snow outside, where he saw a sea of gorgeous, competing evening dresses gliding gracefully over a black and green carpet. Two's joy was complete, but the sight of all those men in suits and patent leather shoes disturbed him. He was a piece of refuse among all the glitter. The sight of his stone-washed jeans among all that finery had them looking daggers.

Zhu Li casually introduced Two to their host as she exchanged lustful glances with him. Two selected his seat with care, a mere arm's length from the buttery cakes, nuts, and chocolates.

"Try one of these," Zhu Li said with uncharacteristic intimacy as she put some sort of preserved fruit into Two's mouth. Of course that was just as the hostess walked regally and stiffly up to them.

The hostess received Two's hand with three limp fingers, her eyes fixed on his delicate hands. There was an awkward pause, as though they were transfixed by the touch of the other's hand. Too bad that all Two could see amid the sparkle of her diamond rings were four little dimples surrounded by delicate softness.

"Which do you prefer, young man, Napoleon or Vat 69?" the hostess asked him in a thin voice, keeping her eyes fixed on him, as though his hands hadn't affected him in the least. But Two, who kept staring at the four meaty hollows amid the sparkle of her diamond rings, froze for a moment before answering. "I don't much like that fellow Napoleon, and I've never heard of Vat 69..."

8

Poor Zhu Li's vanity took a beating with that one, but she managed to keep her anger in check. She nudged Two. "You and your jokes!" She turned to their hostess and gave her a smile dripping with honey. "He likes Ambassador Whiskey."

"Oh, you mean booze!" the surprised Two exclaimed.

The hostess smiled and gave Zhu Li a condescending look.

Two watched the green-eyed game between the two women with relish. He giggled.

After the hostess walked off to get their drinks, Zhu Li hissed at Two, whose smile had vanished, "What was that idiotic giggle all about? Quit making a fool of yourself!"

A tiny hand, surrounded by the glitter of diamonds, reluctantly handed Two a long-stemmed glass. As he took it she brushed her hand with his — maybe intended, maybe not. It was so soft and delicate he tingled all over. Such indescribable joy!

Her victory assured, the smug hostess could be magnanimous. Turning to Zhu Li, she said with sisterly concern, "Your friend seems to feel a little out of place here. Show him around." She left them to entertain her other guests, who were not the Two type. She seemed to float as she walked, a fairy-like movement in her limbs. As the party began to liven up, the other guests, dressed in their finery, lost interest in Two, for whom this liberation was manifested in gluttony, starting with pastries and ending with a feast of nuts. A satisfied belch ended this phase, and began the more sophisticated eating, where taste and texture gained ascendancy. A nut was placed in the mouth to be sucked and nibbled; once the slightly tart outer layer had dissolved, the nut was shifted by the tongue to a spot between the molars, where it was slowly ground to crumbs, and finally to a richly flavored paste that filled the mouth before sliding down the throat and leaving a savory residue behind. The lips were licked clean, and the process was repeated. Needless to say, this sort of leisurely gourmand activity was possible only when

9

hunger had been stilled. The movie began. Two glanced absent-mindedly at the small screen between insertions of nuts, but only for the first ten minutes or so, after which he just sat there somnolently, without moving a muscle. Once the lights were dimmed and the entertainment had begun, Zhu Li ignored Two and his revolting indolent pose, intent on sitting as close to their host as possible, brushing up against his leg to signal her tender feelings and carnal desire. She shook Two awake when the movie ended. His 'phoenix' eyes snapped open to the unexpected glare of bright lights, making him blink.

"Well, ladies and gentlemen, let's hear what you think," the host announced as he unstuck himself from Zhu Li's thigh, his full, round face swaying slightly.

"A technical breakthrough, absolutely original, especially the lovemaking scene. Real food for thought..." A slight man, probably Malay, with a taut, serious face, spoke up, masking his prurient excitement with artsy talk.

"I found the juxtaposition of folk music and modem art to be a guide to cultural understanding. Quite admirable." In a two-minute monologue Zhu Li managed to invent at least ten new terms, although it was demanding work.

"The color, the panning camera, and the shifting utilization of space are the last word..."

"Directing in such a way as to remove all traces of a director isn't something you can learn overnight!"

"The leading lady has the sexiest lips..."

"Come on, tell me what you didn't like," the host announced in the contrite tone of an artist being seduced by flattery.

Flashbulbs popped, electronic flashes winked.

10

Two's bewitching 'phoenix' eyes panned the room as the sea of faces with their forced little smiles held him spellbound.

Let's hear what this gentleman has to say, the host announced patronizingly, giving Two a chance to speak; it was sort of like doling out money to a beggar on Christmas Eve.

Zhu Li nudged Two. Quickly recovering his senses, he shook his head.

"My husband would like to hear what you have to say. Your feelings will surely represent the opinions of your class!" The pudgy hand surrounded by the glitter of diamonds flashed before Two's eyes. He smiled and said, "I liked it."

The host laughed loudly. "Simple, direct. I love that sort of honest, straightforward criticism!" He laid a hand on Two's back. Two leaned forward to move away from the touch of the man's heavy hand.

"Okay, we've heard the refined and the popular reactions. It isn't easy to make a film of that caliber!"

The host reacted to the flattery with a broad smile that masked the sadness in his heart. He knew how phony most of the comments were, but with reporters present, it was all very necessary. Most of all he appreciated Two's honest response. His wife, who understood at once, passed the platter of fruit to Two. But it was so large he couldn't see her tiny, pudgy hands, and he was mortified. Noticing the smug look on the hostess' face, Zhu Li reached out and took a large apple, but stopped just as she was about to bite into it and said matter-of-factly, "These cinematic scholars have seen too many films. By listening to them, you can see that their pursuit of art has returned to its simple origins."

"Aha! The genuine article doesn't show off, the show off isn't the genuine article. It's an honor to be appreciated by an expert and a scholar! Zhu Li, let's get a picture of the three of us, and send it along with your critique to the *Overseas Chinese Daily* for Publisher Lin to use this Sunday. What do you say?"

"Of course, of course."

Zhu Li squeezed in between the two men, put her arm tightly around the host's waist, and gave him a meaningful poke.

Electronic flashes and arc lamps blinded her for a moment as she struck the pose of the world's most beautiful woman seeking the favors of the world's most handsome man.

Utterly disgusted by the scene in front of her, the hostess asked in a voice dripping with sarcasm, "I wonder if our famous movie critic has read the recent obscene novel by that literary scholar you brought with you last time. What was it called? *The Female Corpse Is a Man's Warm Bed* or something like that. If so, what did he think of it?" The hostess was gesturing emotionally, and poor Two's eyes were getting tired following her hands.

The hostess held a dainty finger in front of Two's eyes and asked him mockingly, "Well, tell us, did you *like* it?"

Two stared at the finger in stupefaction before nodding and replying honestly, "Yes."

The first reaction in the room was terror, followed by an explosion of laughter. Two joined in. The host, meanwhile, noticed the seething jealousy of the two women, which threatened to erupt at any minute. Knowing that could only spell trouble, he announced abruptly that the film discussion was over and that it was time to begin the costume ball. People began dressing putting on costumes in imitation of their favorite movie stars. But when the hostess saw that Zhu Li was wearing the costume of an eighteen-year-old maiden, she handed Two the clothes of a hooligan that had been shunned by everyone and said with a smile that hinted at her secret delight, "This is just right for you."

The others loudly voiced their agreement.

Seeing that the hostess was trying to embarrass Two, Zhu Li tried to come to his rescue. But he was as happy as a lark, so she kept her anger bottled up. Two loved having the hostess dress him up in a comical, unsightly costume, while she maliciously decided to comb his hair straight up on top, to which both the host and Zhu Li objected. But Two just knelt meekly in front of the hostess, soaking up the joy of having her tiny hands work on his head, the squint of his bewitching 'phoenix' eyes bearing witness to his contentment. The hostess' humiliating behavior had shattered Zhu Li's plans, and she wished she hadn't brought Two along. She wanted to warn him, but by then he was the center of attention, and the hostess, who was nearly bursting with joy, searched the crowd for Zhu Li. Two stood there like an idiot for a moment, then sprang into action, like a wolf pouncing on its prey, grabbing the hostess' hand and kissing it with extraordinary passion. Caught completely off guard, she tried to pull her hand from his grip, but his lips seemed attached to the four meaty hollows like magnets, and he wasn't about to let go.

The reaction of the other guests, whose curiosity quickly turned to excitement, then mocking laughter, were suddenly frightened by the sight of Two, his body taut and trembling, his face bathed in sweat, seemingly transformed into a savage, rapacious beast. The host pushed his way through the crowd, jerked Two back, and demanded, "What do you think you're doing?"

Two staggered backwards, releasing his grip on the hostess' hand, and stared at the crowd while he wiped his sweaty face, as though he were in a different world. "Wasn't I supposed to play the role someone depraved?"

"Don't get funny with me!" the host bellowed.

Seeing that things had gotten out of hand, Zhu Li grabbed Two and left the party as fast as she could. "What's wrong with you today?" she asked him after they'd turned a distant corner.

13

Two didn't reply. He just kept walking, the only sound the squishing of snow beneath his feet.

"I said what's wrong with you?" Zhu Li demanded, grabbing hold of his sleeve.

Two kicked the snow, which sparkled under the streetlight. He just smiled. "Too bad. What China's missing is a revolting middle class." He removed Zhu Li's hand and walked on, his long legs lacking their usual spring. Faster and faster he moved, until he had left her far behind.

Zhu Li, still puzzled by his comment gnashed her teeth and exclaimed to the white snow gleaming in the night, "Two, you bastard!"

Chapter 2

She didn't say a word to anyone during the sixteen-hour flight. The row behind her was occupied by balding old men talking about genetic engineering and HR factors, their conversation literally reeking of scholarship; their business suits and patent leather shoes made you sweat. Some elderly Caucasian women to her left, sporting bright Great Wall or Temple of Heaven T-shirts, were an explosion of spring blossoms in an ancient forest. A young couple in front, dressed in coarse, tattered cotton shirts, were talking about levels of financial sponsorship and the relative merits of J-1 and F-1 visas with such profound understanding and meticulous analysis that she was reminded of her own painful experience in obtaining the twelve official seals of approval. Her heart froze as she instinctively felt for the brown-covered passport pinned to her underwear.

"Do you speak Chinese, Miss?"

She became aware of the saccharine voice while she was waiting in line for the lavatory. With a hurried glimpse she saw — sensed is probably more like it — a round, pushed-in, eunuch-like face with a beaming smile. As she nodded her gaze characteristically alit on the second button of his jacket, the shine of which reflected her face with distortion. The reflection changed with each movement, long one moment, squat the next, but always with a blinding glint.

"Your first visit to the States?" The voice was so smarmy she lowered her long eyelashes out of a subconscious fear that she'd get stuck in the sugary goo, and a desire to keep from showing her disgust.

"May I know what you're called?"

She smiled and slipped into the lavatory, staying longer than necessary.

15

"Here's my card. Let me know if you have any problems in the States."

The fancy name card was thrust into her hand as she emerged from the lavatory.

A curved index finger with thick knuckles touched the palm of her band; her stomach turned, as though she'd been touched by a fly-spotted piece of rotten sausage, and she could barely keep from throwing up. She looked up into two sparkling little eyes openly scrutinizing her unguarded face. Taking the name card, she rushed back to her seat and gazed out the window at the white clouds floating and curling in the sky beside her.

She awoke at three in the morning, her heart pounding, and tiptoed into the combination washroom-kitchen shared by seven families, where she ran a toothbrush over her teeth a couple of times and washed her face, then rushed outside, jumped onto her bicycle, and rode over to the departure section of the Beijing Public Security Bureau. Two long lines had already formed in the darkness, and they weren't moving. She shivered, experiencing an unnamed fear as her eyes followed the human snakes until they were swallowed up by the night. Bracing herself, she walked up and asked what the two lines were for, then walked to the end of the left-hand line, for people applying to go to Europe and North America. Her fear evaporated once she was in line and surrounded by other people, and the sweat on her body quickly dried in the cool winds whistling through the crowd. Her scalp grew taut and the goosebumps all over her body stubbornly refused to go away even after she'd walked in place for a few moments. She knew that her frail body, conceived out of wedlock by a fifty-eight-year old father and mother, could not withstand this alternating chill and heat, tension and relaxation, and in three or four hours she'd have a cold, with all the attendant fever, runny nose, and headaches. As dawn was about to break, she was tempted to run over to a cafe around the corner for a bowl of hot soybean milk to warm herself but she didn't dare, since the line behind her kept getting longer and longer. She stuck it out till eight-thirty, when a strapping young man and a policewoman who looked

16

like the Goddess of Mercy emerged to open the doors before the two lines. The crowd began to stir. "Not so fast!" someone shouted. "Wait your turn!"

The young policeman was grinning broadly. "How can you be so energetic this early in the morning? How do you expect us to sleep! Hey, you people in line for Japan, Hong Kong, and Macao, the first five can come in. Don't shove! Five at a time!"

"Comrade, do we have to line up to pick up forms?"

"Take it easy, now, get in line." The policeman let five people in, then closed the door behind them.

The line for Europe and North America was half again as long as that for Japan, Hong Kong, and Macao, and it was eleven o'clock before her turn came. The Goddess of Mercy policewoman said in a gentle voice, "Sit closer. Right over here."

Such gratitude filled her heart that she didn't know what sort of humble expression would be appropriate. Ultimately, as always, she rested her eyes on the second button of the policewoman's coat.

"Are you here to turn in a form or pick one up?"

"Pick one up. Family visit. My husband's a student in the States."

"Ah, all the husbands and children abroad seem to be students these days. Your documents?"

"Here's a sponsorship certificate from my aunt. And here's my husband's I-20."

The middle-aged policewoman looked the form over, then smiled affectionately and said, "I can't give you your form yet."

Her eyelids shot up in alarm. The stout policewoman squirmed in her squeaky chair, her broad hips seemingly obliterating all her hopes.

"We still need a letter of invitation from your husband and certification from both your and your husband's work units approving the visit. Everything has to be complete before we can issue the form."

Every joint in her body seemed to fill up with ice water, and she had a sneezing fit that made her ears ring. All that paperwork for a measly form? You don't know what it took to get these two letters. God knows how many bodhisattvas and earth gods I'll have to call on before I can get the rest. She was tired and scared.

"Next. Sit closer. Ah, right there." The Goddess of Mercy policewoman, unmoved by the dejected look on her face, turned to the next person in line with the same gentle voice.

"Why *not give* me a form now, and I'll turn it in for examination with all the necessary documents when it's complete? Wouldn't that save time and trouble?" she asked timidly as she stood up to give her seat to the next person in line.

The policewoman replied in the same gentle, intimate tone, "Can't do that. Procedures, you know."

She sneezed again and her scalp tightened. Her temples throbbed painfully. She had more questions, but was afraid of giving the policewoman a bad impression, which could make things hard for her when she came back; she swallowed her words.

"Shan Naiwo, remember, the documents need to be signed by a section chief or higher!"

The policewoman added a final comment as she was on her way out the door. She stepped out into the blinding sunlight, where

18

the two lines were squirming like a hen trying to lay an oversized egg. She felt terrible, saw spots in front of her eyes.

"Is something wrong, Miss?"

That gave her a start. Her eyes snapped open and immediately affixed themselves on the second button of a powder blue stewardess uniform. She shook her head.

"You can turn off the overhead light and close the window shade if you want to sleep. Would you like a blanket?"

She shook her head again.

The first person she saw when she stepped off the airplane was her husband. A powerful sense of unfamiliarity stopped her in her tracks. She spotted the loathsome "phoenix eyes" at once, but could barely recognize the little frame inside the stone-washed jeans as the man whose bed she'd shared, the one with whom she had a love-hate relationship.

Without a trace of affection or hesitation, he took her carry-on bag from her and pushed his way up to the baggage carousel. "What color's your luggage?" he asked her. "What color?"

The low spirits that had weighed her down for so long vanished as a result of his bustle; without giving herself a chance to feel gratitude or shed tears of complaint, she joined him by the carousel to look for her luggage. There was a heavy stillness in the humid night air. Spinning streetlights lit up a dark little car, a beam of cold, eerie light. As she walked behind Two, who was carrying a suitcase in each hand, she was so lightheaded she felt as though she were still up in the sky. He'd parked so far away that her arms were growing numb from the weight of her carry-on bags. She wondered if they'd ever get to where they were going. All sorts of scenarios of their meeting had gone through her mind, but this sort of stupefying bustle hadn't been one of them. Another spectral beam of light flashed before her eyes; this one seemed hot, and she held her breath

19

to keep her tears back. Back in the cadre office she hadn't been able to stem the flood of tears, to her everlasting humiliation.

Serious business is conducted in a political department's cadre office. "Try to think like a soldier. Go outside if you're going to cry!" a clerk on temporary assignment from Zhejiang bellowed at her. She had no idea why, since he didn't know her and couldn't conceivably have anything against her; but there was loathing in his eyes, and he'd started making things hard on her the minute she handed him her exit application form.

"Soldiers are people, too, and tears don't know a political department from any other place," she replied tearfully, feeling unbearably wronged.

"Go outside and cry! I said this is a political department. How would it look to have a bunch of crybabies around the place?"

"You have no right to tell me to leave! And no right to lie to me! I know my application has been in your drawer all this time, so why'd you lie to me and say you sent it to the deputy commissar days ago?"

"You have no right to go over my head to the deputy commissar. Your only right is to trust the organization and the Party!"

"How can I trust an organization or a party that allows this?"

"Okay, fine! You say you can't trust the organization or the Party? Write that down, write it down, I say!" The skinny little clerk, suddenly feeling his oats, ran out from behind his desk and stood in front of her, thrusting pen and paper into her hand.

She shuddered, as though she were standing in the middle of a Cultural Revolution denunciation session. But she gave him a scornful look and said in the coldest manner possible, "How can something like you be produced in this day and age?"

20

"*Something* like me? A proper member of the Communist Party, a clerk in the political department? Let me tell you, there are plenty of enlightened people like me around! You so-called cultural people couldn't look like real soldiers on your dying day! You could be declared a counterrevolutionary for what you just said, and there wouldn't be a goddamned thing you could do about it! Allowing someone like you out of the country is just turning people loose who'd sell out their own country!"

"Not to worry. Where in the world could you find a buyer for a backward country like this?"

She was so angry she shook. No tears this time.

"Are you cold? Why are you shivering? Hurry up. If I park longer than an hour it'll cost me another two bucks." All Two wanted was to get her moving again.

She couldn't stop shivering, and her teeth were chattering so hard she couldn't speak. Two unlocked the door and put the luggage in the back seat, then jumped into the driver's seat and wiped the torn passenger seat with his sleeve before she climbed in, then helped her with her seatbelt.

This so warmed her heart she nearly cried. The tough exterior of the heart of a woman long denied the comforting presence of a man is more fragile, more sensitive than most.

"If a cop sees you without a seatbelt he'll give me a ticket. Since they have nothing else to do, Salt Lake City cops spend all their time worrying about piddling things like that." Assured that her seatbelt was properly fastened, he started the engine.

Thousands of miles and all that trouble for a greeting like this? Her heart grew heavier and heavier, until there was no more feeling at all; she felt numb. The sputtering of the engine and all the other racket made by the pickup truck reminded her that she had

21

abandoned all her security to come to this unfamiliar place. Gripping the door handle tightly, she kept her eyes fixed on the cars whizzing past them, just as she'd looked at the shiny red official seal in Party Secretary Wang's hand. How much more torment would she have to endure before he'd reach down and affix the seal to the letter approving her overseas visit? She was tempted to beg him, or play up to him, or promise to give him some sort of gift; but then she remembered her determination to trust her luck and not cave in to anybody.

"How many years has your husband been abroad?" Secretary Wang asked as he adjusted his thick reading glasses.

"Three. Wait a minute, let me think. She hesitated. If I tell him the truth and say three and a half, he'll say his time's up and he should return home. If I say less than two, he'll say it's only been a little over a year, so what's your hurry?" She thought it over carefully before saying two years.

"Does the college president approve?"

She mopped her brow, which she realized was beaded with sweat, then stood up.

"I'll go see him."

"He's away on business."

"When will he be back?"

"The twentieth of next month."

"The twentieth?" She sat down again, dejected, deflated, lowering her long lashes to cover up the look of desperation in her eyes.

"As luck would have it, the vice-president's away, too," Secretary Wang said as he turned the seal over in his hand and

22

cleaned some of the dried ink out of the indentations with a thumbtack.

With a sigh of resignation she said, "It's like having a layer of skin scraped away for each official seal I need to get. Now another hitch!"

"What do you mean, another hitch?" Secretary Wang breathed on the seal he'd finished cleaning and placed it down in perfect alignment on the letter, which had only two lines of text.

Her first reaction was "It couldn't possibly be that easy." Her second was that Secretary Wang had something in mind. She braced herself for an obscene proposition or a demand for some material incentive.

"Foreigners are puzzled over how husbands and wives can put up with being separated for long periods," Secretary Wang said with a smile as he pressed down on the seal, then blew on the ink to quicken the drying process. What a pitiful, comical character I am, she suddenly felt. I've been living in odious surroundings so long I've forgotten how to accept anything that's done with relative ease. She looked up and scrutinized Secretary Wang's face: wrinkled, pale, the same disagreeable expression whether he was laughing or crying. She grabbed his hands and shook them long and hard, mumbling over and over, "I wouldn't have believed it, I simply wouldn't have believed it!"

"Local institutions and the military are different, especially an art institute like ours. We're happy to oblige anyone who's deserving of going abroad."

She took the letter and backed over to the door, her heart filled with a gratitude she was incapable of expressing, feelings that were still with her as she stood in line at the Public Security Bureau the next morning, where she was told that her form was ready — just like that. That made her uncomfortable, put her on guard. They sent her to the carefree young policeman in charge of paperwork for requests to go to Europe and North America, where she respectfully handed him the documents she'd obtained at the cost of nervous tension, anxiety, and lots of tears. Since he was on the phone, he rested the receiver on his shoulder to continue his chatty conversation with the person on the other end, reached into a drawer, and took out the two-page application form along with a stack of official letters he hadn't so much as glanced at; handing it all to her, he raised a finger to indicate that she owed one yuan for administrative fees. The ease of it all trimmed her mental preparation from two feet thick to the thickness of a piece of paper that was worth — nothing. Her feelings of sheer good luck and hostility evaporated in an instant, although her sense of having been wronged and her feelings of sorrow hung on tenaciously. A person's fate, she reasoned, was like a cheap communal toy at the mercy of whichever child was playing with it, and who could discard it at will. She felt like shouting at the young man, Don't you people know how to respect others? But he'd just think she was off her rocker and incapable of appreciating a favor, someone getting angry because she'd gotten her way. Besides, there were plenty of things in her past that this young man or others like him could use to make trouble for her, and just thinking of the consequences of offending them was more than she could bear. Once she was out the door she realized she'd crumpled the forms in her hand.

"Eat something, then get some sleep. I have to go to work." Two put a glass of cold milk and some bread on the table in front of her.

"So late? What kind of job?"

"Cleaning the classrooms and bathrooms. Every night, from ten till two in the morning. Four bucks an hour. I'm already an hour late tonight."

"You've been here over three years, so why are you still cleaning bathrooms?"

"I like the job. Nobody's around, so I don't have to talk to anybody. I get paid for four hours, but it only takes me an hour, so I have three hours to read or think."

"Why not get a job in a Chinese restaurant or in the library?"

"I've done that. Go ahead and eat. I have to go. What's the difference?"

"What's the difference? Don't slap your face to make yourself look well fed. Is there no difference between cleaning bathrooms and designing spacecraft?"

Two had a far-off look in his eyes, and she couldn't tell if he was looking at her or at the wall behind her. "You haven't changed a bit," he said timidly.

"No matter how much I changed I'd never turn into a useless piece of goods like you."

He left with smirking.

Instead of eating she took a look around Two's little room. It was old and rundown, but the rug, the telephone, and the bathroom and kitchen were fine; he had everything he needed. She filled the tub and slipped in to soak in the hot, bubbly water, which quickly washed away the exhaustion of her long trip. She was reminded of a foreign movie in which a bath like this was the female lead's greatest pleasure. The thought of Two enjoying himself like this came as a surprise to her.

"Not bad," she muttered to herself.

"What do you mean, not bad? The last tenant left it behind." Two was standing in the bathroom doorway.

25

"Oh, you scared me! What are you doing back so soon?" Overcome by a sense of strangeness and shyness, she covered her exposed breasts with a towel.

"Your flight was an hour late, and since I didn't ask for time off, the boss got someone to take my place." Two looked out the window into the dark sky as he sat on the floor next to the tub. He sighed and said, "Now what?"

"What do you mean, now what?"

"Now that you're here, what do we do? I don't make enough to support two people, so if you're going to stay you'll have to find a job. Some Chinese restaurants are willing to pay under the table, and the only other possibility is babysitting. But if you get caught..." if he said anything more, she didn't hear it, for she was caught up in anger.

"I wrote and told you not to come now, but you insisted. God, this is worse than being in China..."

"That's enough!" She rolled over and put her head underwater, not surfacing until her heart was racing wildly. She spat out a mouthful of soapy water and tears. Two sat there like a statue staring at the faucet. "You're an evil man!" she said through clenched teeth.

"I'm just telling the truth. Maybe you should..."

"I should put as much distance as possible between me and your black bones right away!" Forgetting everything but her anger, she stood up. Two stared at her naked body, warily, wanting to go up to her, but not daring to. He finally picked up the towel and gingerly wrapped it around her. "In the States overseas Chinese students are the cheapest commodity," he said dully, "especially male students from the mainland studying humanities without a scholarship. Give yourself some time to decide whether or not you want to leave me..."

She brushed his hands away and dressed quickly, then took out the name card and read it, her mind suddenly a blank. Now that she'd left her homeland and was in a place she'd barely had a chance to see, she didn't know whom to look up, who to depend upon, except Two. She had a schoolmate at NYU, but she had her own problems and wouldn't be able to help. Her aunt was well off, but she'd made it clear that her guarantee of financial support was only a formality, and that she'd have to make her own way in the States. Who else was there? She looked up; there was sympathy in Two's 'phoenix' eyes. Disgust, shame and resentment, self esteem, and a ton of grievances filled her heart like a huge lump. She wasn't about to give him the satisfaction of thinking she was wavering or feeling awkward, and even less willing to let him think she needed him, that he was her only hope.

"There's nothing I can do..."

"Since there's nothing you can do, I'll just go off and die. But don't think I'll do it here in front of you."

"You're a woman, you can't speak the language, and American society's a mess, with hooligans and bad people all over the place."

"I can't imagine anybody being a bigger hooligan than you, or any worse. I'd be better off working as some pimp's whore than your wife! All I ask of you is never to hear your voice again." While she was voicing every angry thought in her mind, like a blinding light the word hooligan reminded her of that smarmy, sugary voice that seemed to get all her stuck in goo. Reaching into her pocket, she took out the name card, walked over to the telephone, and dialed the number. Once, twice... each time an operator's voice came on the line, but she didn't understand a word.

Two handed her a note: "You have to dial '1' for a long-distance number. It's cheaper if you call after eleven PM."

27

She pushed the note away in disgust and bellowed in exasperation, "I'm paying!" The shrillness of her voice ripped through the still night, a desolate, desperate sound. She felt like she was burning up. Just as she was about to slam down the receiver, the number she had dialed began to ring. But the second she heard that smarmy, sugary voice, she regretted her impetuous behavior. And yet standing there in front of Two, for some strange reason she felt an intimacy with that repulsive voice. Everything went more smoothly than she had any right to hope, for he agreed to help over the phone. But when she hung up the phone her heart felt as though it were tied in knots, and she had a premonition that the worst was yet to come. All the reasons why she should be relieved ran through her mind, but her fears actually increased. She started crying, feeling as sad as she'd ever felt, like a girl who'd just been deflowered.

Chapter 3

Big Jimmy. Jianmin is one of the most common names among students from China, and most of them choose the Western name Jimmy. In order to avoid confusion, they often add the words big, or small, or fat, or skinny. Well, Big Jimmy sort of passed his broom over the classrooms, followed that with the vacuum cleaner wherever he could see some dirt, then hid out in the spacious women's bathroom to loaf, since it was the safest place. The janitor, a clever Jewish fellow, could easily find you no matter where you hid, except in the women s bathroom. Even though there were no students inside at nighttime, he still knocked on the door or called out Hello, then asked politely, Jimmy, are you in there? Jimmy would open the door, holding a wastepaper basket or a wet mop. Big Jimmy was really tired tonight, mentally and physically. His passport was about to expire, even though he hadn't completed his studies, and he'd had no word since leaving it at the consulate. Then his advisor had told him this morning that his scholarship wouldn't be renewed next year, since they'd given the course entitled "The Influence of the *Book of Changes* on Eastern Literature" to Zhu Li, which in simple terms meant that even if his passport was renewed, the only way he'd be able to continue his studies was to clean classrooms and school bathrooms every night to pay for his tuition. At noon he'd gone to the computer to knock off two papers that were due tomorrow, drunk a glass of cold water, and run over to the American's house where his wife babysat to pick her up and take her to the hospital for a checkup. Before he reached the parking lot he spotted her standing beside his car signaling him with her head.

"Why are you early?"

She frowned without answering him.

After an examination and some lab tests, the doctor wrote on the chart "early stages of pregnancy, about two and a half months." There was a consultation, some forms were signed, then the doctor agreed to perform an abortion. Big Jimmy took out the health insurance certificate he'd gotten the day before and handed it to the blonde, gray-eyed cashier, who smiled and said sympathetically, "I'm sorry, but if you'll read the fourth clause you'll see that patients with chronic illnesses, tumors, or pregnancies are required to apply for coverage two months before the first medical visit. If you want the surgery performed you'll have to pay seven hundred dollars."

Big Jimmy leaned weakly up against the wall and said, completely demoralized; "I just wasted thirty bucks on health insurance!"

The blonde, gray-eyed cashier gave him a friendly smile and said apologetically, "I'm sorry, I don't understand Japanese or Chinese."

Big Jimmy smiled a weak, sad smile and shook his head. Once he'd calmed down he realized how hungry he was. His wife was bent over a spittoon with the dry heaves, shaking her head back and forth in agony, but instead of going over and holding her or saying something to make her feel better, he stared at the snack-dispensing machine in the corner, walked over and inserted a couple of coins, and pushed the button for popcorn. After wolfing down the whole bag, he spotted his wife stumbling out the door. As he caught up with her and was about to say something to make her feel better, it seemed a big waste of time, so he kept his mouth shut.

The dry heaves returned, and her eyes filled with tears.

"I'll drive you to work. We'll think of something."

She held her hand to her chest and rested her head on his shoulder, shaking it gently.

"Take some time off? A few days' rest is all you need."

She shook her head again without raising it from his shoulder.

"You don't mean..." Big Jimmy stopped walking and looked at his wife, who was still pretty green around the gills. "You need a few days' rest," he said, more for his own benefit than for hers.

"I'm not going back."

"Did they fire you?"

"They only hired me because the old guy was in poor health and low spirits. But he can't eat when I'm throwing up all the time... I asked them to let me work a few days more, but they said no..."

Big Jimmy put his arms around her, even though his heart was tied up in knots. Suddenly feeling that her suffering was finally being appreciated, she walked home in his arms like a sickly child, where he gently coaxed her to sleep.

Zhu Li had a new haircut, with girlish bangs to cover up the wrinkles on her forehead and give her an innocent, high-school look. Of course, that was only if you were a couple of meters or more away from her. Close up the impression was of a much older woman trying to look young, and not doing a very good job of it. She stood there, her firm breasts jutting up under her blouse, asking to borrow a hair dryer.

"It's broken," a flustered Big Jimmy said to get her to leave.

"I can fix it," she said coquettishly, fluttering her tiny eyes set in a sea of dark blue and pushing her breasts up close to him. "Is it the same one I used before?" she asked softly.

Big Jimmy motioned toward the bedroom, then said loudly, "Ling, would you like some water?"

"No, thanks," came his wife's weak reply.

Zhu Li shrugged her shoulders mockingly and said in a normal voice, "Would you mind looking for it for me?"

31

Big Jimmy had no choice but to go into the bathroom and open the cabinet, sending a bunch of cockroaches scurrying for cover. He picked up a can of insect repellant and sprayed the area.

Zhu Li followed him into the bathroom. "Well? Was your passport extended?" Big Jimmy sprayed like crazy without deigning to reply.

"If you've already had a year's extension it's hard to get a second one. A bunch of students on J-1 visas sent a joint letter to China recently, asking the government to revoke the policy of forcing them to return upon graduation to work for two years."

"Let's change the subject." He tossed the used-up can of insect repellant noisily into the wastebasket, found the hair dryer, and handed it to Zhu Li, who cast a quick glance into the bedroom, grabbed his hand, and gave him a tender, affectionate look. Big Jimmy disgustedly tried to pull his hand free and said in a low voice, "What do you want from me?" "Out with it, don't act like that! What have I ever done to you?" she asked softly. "It's only been a few months since we broke up. How could you forget so fast?"

"We needed what we had back then, but don't expect me to hurt my wife." He jerked his hand free with such force that the hair dryer crashed to the floor. They froze and looked toward the bedroom. Zhu Li laughed mockingly and said in a normal, composed voice, "Sorry, I dropped your hair dryer."

Big Jimmy looked at her gratefully and said apologetically, "Everything's gone wrong lately." He backed out of the bathroom like he was avoiding the plague. Then, raising his voice, he said, "My passport expires next month. If I don't get an extension I'll have to go back. A billion people get by somehow, so what's there to be afraid of?"

Zhu Li sneered. "What's there to be afraid of? How about not being able to use what you learned? How about all those complex

32

personal relationships? How about the possibility that your wife won't get transferred to Shanghai? How about squeezing three people into twelve square feet of living space?"

Big Jimmy just stared at her dumbly without saying a thing.

Zhu Li walked up and rested her hand on his shoulder, saying to him with a tenderness that flowed like water, "Well, life goes on. A couple of years of under-the-table wages will get you ten thousand dollars or so, which is all you'll need for the rest of your life over there. The black-market rate is seven to one, so you'll be a lot better off than people who get by on a paycheck. I'm having a party tonight. Bring your wife over."

"I'm not in your league. You get a full scholarship for next year, while I have to clean bathrooms every night. I'm in no mood for a party."

"Oh, so that's it..." Zhu Li walked out the door mumbling to herself, then tuned and gave him the eye one last time.

Big Jimmy, more confused than ever, didn't notice the look as he threw himself down on the sofa, closed his eyes, and mulled over the problem of his wife's abortion. After a while, she came in with a steaming bowl of noodles and gently nudged him awake. "You haven't eaten all day, have you?"

Big Jimmy took the bowl from her. When all is said and done it's my wife who really cares about me, he thought to himself.

His wife sat on the floor next to him and rested her hands weakly on his knees, her head lowered, without speaking.

Big Jimmy slurped his noodles.

"I don't blame you," she blurted out.

33

Big Jimmy sprang into a sitting position, spilling hot noodles on his hand. He shook it hard.

"You were all alone the first two years, and I know how hard it was for you. You needed a woman like that for a little relief and she needed a man to help her out in a place like this. Don't treat her like that. I feel sorry for her. It's not as though nothing happened..."

Big Jimmy looked nervously at the understanding look in his wife's eyes and wavered momentarily. But he said nothing.

She picked up their daughter's photograph from the tea table and wiped off the dust with her hand, "If it weren't for her," she said softly, "I'd let the two of you..."

"That's crazy!" He slurped down the remaining noodles and put down the bowl, disgustedly flipping off a noodle that had stuck to his hand. "Instead of spouting a bunch of nonsense you should be thinking about where we can get the money for an abortion, how we can get our daughter over, how I can get my passport extended so I can finish my studies."

She began vomiting again, yellow bile spurting from her nose.

Big Jimmy frowned, put on his jacket, and walked outside, where the cold wind hit his face and neck like daggers. It was cold, and he hurt.

Two girls in short skirts and high boots brushed past him, looking as though the cold didn't bother them a bit. He observed inwardly that girls who have grown up on steak are certainly different.

The girls gave him a friendly greeting, "Happy Thanksgiving!"

No wonder there were so many cars and pedestrians out on a cold, snowy night like this! He strolled aimlessly past a luxury home nestled among some snow-covered pines. A dog the size of a small bear fell silently in behind him and brushed its nose up against his leg. His heart nearly stopped, but he quickly composed himself and stood there without moving, keeping his eyes on the animal.

The dog's mouth was no more than an inch from his leg when a fat old lady stuck her head through the gate and shouted, "Come, my dear." Hearing its mistress' command, the bear-like dog called off the attack and bounded over to her like a well-behaved child. Too bad, Big Jimmy thought. Her command had cheated him out of enough medical expenses, living costs, and damages for pain and suffering to last him the rest of his life. Being bitten by a dog in America is the same as taking a bite out of the bank. With this thought on his mind, he turned and looked back at the old woman, who was showering affection on the dog. That bright smiling face of hers had probably never been marred by lines of tears. An inexpressible sense of shame quickly filled his heart. He closed his eyes and began running through the blowing snow.

The sound of screeching brakes and loud curses jolted him back to his senses. He looked up at the car in front of him and said, "Oops, sorry." His heart was pounding.

"Shut up!" the bearded driver shot back, his eyes nearly popping out of his head. He glared a moment longer, then slammed the car into gear and drove off, sending snow and ice flying.

Big Jimmy cursed him back, although he wasn't sure if it was meant for the bearded driver or for himself.

"Hello! Jimmy, are you in there?" the janitor said through the door of the women's bathroom after knocking.

Big Jimmy opened the door holding a wastebasket in his hand.

"You can knock off now, Jimmy. Go wash up. Here, have a beer. You shouldn't be working like this on Thanksgiving."

35

Big Jimmy breathed a sigh of relief and took the pop-top can of beer and a slice of turkey. They clinked beer cans solemnly in the doorway of the women's bathroom, as the janitor raised his flushed face and bloodshot eyes heavenward and said with the passion of a woman in love, "Thank you, Lord, for allowing our forefathers, who came from the four corners of the earth, to pass their first winter in peace. That's why we use the Indians' favorite food — turkey — to show our thanks. Amen!" With that he tipped back his bead and chug-a-lugged the can of beer. He mumbled another Thank you, turned, and left Big Jimmy standing there alone.

Big Jimmy didn't know what to do now. He didn't feel like working any more, but hated the thought of going home to listen to his wife throw up. So he sat down on one of the clean sinks, lit a Marlboro, and blew a series of smoke rings. Then he flipped through an old copy of *People's Daily*. The headline "Increased Restrictions on Second Children" caught his eye. A devilish scheme suddenly formed in his mind, and his heart skipped a beat. He jumped down off of the sink and looked into the mirror. "Good idea!" he exclaimed with a loud snap of his finger.

Chapter 4

On Saturday night Big and Little Jimmy invited Zhu Li to go with them to a new casino that had just opened in Las Vegas; if they got four people altogether, each paying $200, they'd be entitled to $900 worth of chips and coupons and a chance to win a digital clock, a camera, or a VCR. Based upon their calculations of probability and permutations, they thought their chances of winning were pretty good. Zhu Li was moved, not by the chances of winning, but by the fact that Big Jimmy, who had been in a terrible mood lately, had shown enough interest to invite her. She'd never forgotten that when she first arrived, with a TOEFL score under 550, she'd been denied admission into the Department of Far Eastern Languages, and that he'd taken her to see his advisor and introduced her as a specialist in the *Book of Changes* and Zen Buddhism. He'd even offered to write to experts in China for letters of recommendation. His advisor, moved to sympathy, broke precedent by accepting her into the graduate program. Nor had she forgotten the time she was sick, with no one to take care of her, no health insurance, and no money to see a doctor, how he had given her moral support and nursed her back to health as attentively as if she were his own wife; she'd not only regained her health because of him, but her self-confidence in the process. Most of all, she'd never forget that morning when he'd gotten out of her bed to go to the airport to meet his wife's plane and said agonizingly, "We can't be together after today. I know you want to marry a U.S. citizen or a permanent resident so you won't have to work like a slave just to get by. And I don't plan to get a divorce..." unable to go on, he turned and walked out the door like a man who'd lost a piece of his heart. The thought of marrying him had never crossed her mind, but neither had the thought of losing him. He was the only person who understood her and did what she asked. On the surface, Zhu Li, a thirty-three-year-old woman who seemingly refused to grow up, came across as someone whose feminine emotions and appearance hadn't progressed beyond the stage of young maidenhood, and who believed that men had been put on this world to serve and dote on her. In reality, however, people generally saw her as a silly little plaything, flattering and praising her as a prank;

38

and she always fell for it, feeling better and better all the time. At times like this, they'd be moved by how dense she was and how pure her feelings were, and would treat her as a foolish, lovable little thing with whom they could let down their guard. Big Jimmy was the only who knew that while this was a part of her personality, to some degree she was like this on purpose; a complex woman, she wasn't all that easy to understand. Sometimes even she didn't know why she was frequently powerless to keep from playing the fool, but most of the time she was simply and genuinely intoxicated by the manipulative flattery. Yet late at night, when all was quiet, she'd feel the deep-seated pain and resolve to change her frivolous ways. But as soon as it was light again, or as soon as she met a man who could be useful to her or whom she found attractive, she'd forget her resolve and once again feel and act like an eighteen-year-old girl.

Tonight the happiness returned. Big Jimmy had invited her to make up a party of four, and a trip like this couldn't help but improve things between the two of them. She started calling around, but everyone was either out or busy. Reluctantly, she thought of Two, since he was her last chance to make up the required number. As she dialed his number, she worried that he might not be a gambler. When she explained the situation, he said simply, "I'll think it over," and hung up. Figuring it was hopeless, she tried everybody she could think of, but still came up empty, and was sure she'd miss this opportunity. Then the phone. It was Two. "I'll go. What time?"

"All we need is the right number of people."

"Can you give me a couple of hours?"

"Sure. Meet at my place in two hours. We'll take my car and split the gas."

Two surprised them by showing up a half-hour late, loaded down with bread, lunchmeat, fruit, and soft drinks. They felt like laughing, but, knowing his temper, pretended not to notice and ignored him. Twenty minutes into their trip Two was snoring so loudly no one else could sleep. The sight of him sleeping, with his

39

legs curled up, his mouth open and slobbering, and his head lolling up against Zhu Li, was more than they could take. Zhu Li nudged him annoyingly; he opened his bewitching 'phoenix' eyes and looked around, but as soon as he saw that no one was paying him any attention, he quickly fell back to sleep. At four in the morning they pulled into the casino parking lot and decided to leave Two in the car while they went in to get something to eat, planning to come back and wake him up after they were finished. But before they could put their plan into action, an alarm clock in Two's pocket went off and woke him up. He jumped out of the car, stretched, and took out a loaf of bread. Want something to eat? he asked them, then dug in. The others went ahead and ate a simple meal, then entered the casino, where they split up their chips. Two was off like a shot to the slot machines, where he carefully fished out two coins with tiny holes drilled in them to which he had tied nearly invisible threads. After assuring himself that no one was watching, he dropped one of the coins into the slot and pulled the handle: once, twice, ten times, always using the same two coins. He settled down and patiently pulled the handle over a hundred times before a hundred or more wins came tumbling noisily into the pan, drawing the attention of a grossly fat woman nearby, who stuck her bead over greedily, scaring Two into shielding his machine with his back. Once the fat woman went back to her own gambling, Two started in again, casually pulling the handle several hundred more times. Finally, whistles sounded, bells rang, and a flood of coins came pouring out of the machine. Without stopping to look at the screen or scoop up his winnings, he pulled out his threaded coin and hid it in his undershirt. Everyone around him turned to look when the whistles sounded, and a casino security guard strolled up, patted him on the shoulder, and said "Good luck! That's a three-hundred-dollar jackpot."

The frightened Two walked over to the cashier with his backpack crammed full of coins and cashed them in. Then he took a turn around the casino, stopping to try his hand at the various games along the way before slipping into the men's room, where he removed the threads from the coins, washed his hands and face, and emerged like a police dog on the alert. He then headed to the blackjack tables, where he sat down on the end stool at a table with a

40

variety of women gamblers. He put down two dollars on the first hand, and lost. Then he bet four dollars, and lost. Then eight dollars... doubling his bet each time. He finally won it back on one hand, then came back with another two-dollar bet. Several hours later, he was only slightly ahead, and not very happy about that. He got up and went into the men's room, where he washed his hands and face again, gargled to clear his throat, and reemerged a new man, full of confidence. He sat down at a table with some Caucasian women, and his lucky streak began: two dollars turned into four, then eight, then sixteen... after every winning hand he let the whole thing ride on the next; he was on a roll, and before long he had stacks of $50 chips piled up in front of him. The dealer called a pit boss over, who stood there watching the game, along with a crowd of curious onlookers who had gathered around the table. As he looked down at his colorful stacks of chips, Two felt his palms itch and his heart beat wildly. He sensed the presence of the crowd around him, but didn't hear a sound except for some heavy breathing directly behind him; he could feel the warmth of the breath. Two was sweating heavily, his eyes were bulging, and a cold shiver ran from his head all the way down to his toes. Feeling as though his head was about to explode, he pushed $1,000 in chips out onto the felt table in front of him, then sat there rigidly, holding his breath as the cards were dealt.

"Blackjack! It's a blackjack!" someone behind him, sounding like Zhu Li, shouted excitedly in Chinese. He froze momentarily and stared at the cards in his hand until Big Jimmy shoved him in the back, and he shakily laid down the cards face up. After the dealer slid his winnings over, he made as if to let it all ride on the next hand, like a conditioned reflex. But Zhu Li reached out and stopped him. "Are you out of your mind?" she shouted in his ear. "Let's get out of here!"

"What the fuck are you doing?" Two's face changed, as his eyes seemed about to pop out of his head. He pushed her hand away roughly, determined to bet the whole amount, but she reached out and grabbed his hand again, refusing to let go, refusing to let him bet it all no matter how much he struggled and shouted. Big and Little Jimmy took advantage of the struggle to stuff Two's chips into his

41

backpack, just as a security guard and one of the pit bosses came running over. Big Jimmy smiled and said politely, "They're married, and he has a mental problem. She's afraid he'll do something foolish..."

"Trouble?" the security guard asked the dumbfounded dealer.

Regaining his composure, the dealer said, missing the point of the question, "Them Chinese sure like to gamble."

The security guard shrugged his shoulders, said "Good Luck," and walked off.

The pit boss glared at the dealer and said, "Take a break."

Shrugging his shoulders to show it didn't make any difference to him, the dealer handed the cards to another dealer.

After Two's three companions had cashed in his winnings of four thousand dollars, they dragged him like a kidnap victim over to the motel where they were staying. Big and Little Jimmy undressed him and carded him into the bathroom, where they put him in the tub to soak for half an hour. After climbing out of the tub, as wrinkled as a prune, he flopped down on the bed and slept as though he were dead, while his companions sat around the bed discussing how to keep him from going into the casino, tossing around the idea of spiriting him into the car while he was asleep and taking him home. After about the time it takes to eat a meal, Two rolled over and woke up, but before he could make it to the door, they rushed over to block his way. He just giggled and shook his head. "Now that we've got money," he said casually, "why not move into a nicer place?" After a prolonged exchange of glances, they convinced themselves that he was okay now, and were soon laughing and talking excitedly about how they'd seized the opportunity and how clever and daring they'd been; all except Two, who stared at them timidly as they pranced around exultantly, trying to outdo one another with their exploits. When they'd calmed down, they moved into the number one luxury resort — Caesar's Palace — where they treated themselves to a delicious Chinese meal. Then Zhu Li had an idea: "Let's take in a show. Two's treat!" Two didn't object. So the four of them, having eaten and drunk their fill, took a table up front to enjoy the extravaganza.

The apricot yellow screen parted slowly, like water, like lips, in front of a stage bathed in mellow lights: water like a stream flowing beneath the moon's rays on a spring night, lips like a maiden's first kiss. Two hundred lovely showgirls, all the same height and with virtually identical figures, some black and some white, danced out onto the stage, their bodies covered only by flimsy, feathery costumes, like naked truth. All of a sudden, the revolving stage above the customers' tables was filled with a splendid vista of thighs and breasts! They were all but naked, row upon row of them, and yet it was a sacred scene, not blasphemous. After a flurry of jiggling breasts and dancing thighs, the showgirls, all two hundred of them, black and white, spun around and began to gyrate and sway their hips, filling the stage with a forest, with an ocean, with fleshy mounds of lovely buttocks.

"Wow! Where did they ever find so many gorgeous women?" Zhu Li asked Two impulsively, putting her head close to his.

Two's eyes fairly shone and his neck was craned forward like a turtle's, taut and rigid. After a moment he murmured, only half-joking, "You'd never get an eyeful like this in China." "Tsk-tsk."

"Look at him. Like all he wants to do is bury his face in all that feminine flesh up there!" There was often a smutty sound to the thirty-year-old bachelor Little Jimmy's words.

"And I suppose you don't like it?" Big Jimmy commented without taking his eyes off the stage.

"I like it, but you don't see me drooling like that. I used to think only men had lust in their eyes. But look at Zhu Li," Little Jimmy said.

Two took out a pair of opera glasses to bring the buttocks up close, no matter how many there were, male, female, whatever, zooming in one after the other. He shouted his approval at every spectacular jiggle, unmindful of what anyone thought. "Damn, when you think about it, not one of those papers we write can compare with a single pair of those buttocks up on that stage!"

His companions laughed so hard they disturbed the people around them.

Two sat there with his head thrust rigidly forward, as though he were the only person on earth, his eyes flashing, his mouth hanging open, his feelings revealed for all to see.

"Try not to give people the wrong impression of Chinese," Big Jimmy said, keeping his eyes fixed on the stage.

"Nothing in the world can hold a candle to those bodies up there," Two commented to the others as they were walking out. "Let's go again," he pleaded.

"There are other shows," Zhu Li said, taking Two's hand. "Wow, your hand's like ice! Don't let your soul fly off."

"Did you guys notice that they were all wearing transparent stockings?" Two turned to ask Zhu Li with a blank look on his face.

"What difference does it make what they were wearing? You always go overboard." Tired? Big Jimmy patted Two's bony shoulders.

Two nodded and said he was; but that he still wanted to take in another show.

"Since you can barely walk after seeing all those women, maybe we ought to send for your wife and let her try to satisfy your appetite," Little Jimmy said.

44

"It wouldn't be the same," Two said artlessly.

With the lights off and everything in place it's the same.

"You ought to get married or find a girlfriend, so you can get your mind out of the gutter," Zhu Li said as she nudged Little Jimmy.

"I'm no worse than the rest of you," Little Jimmy looked at Big Jimmy out of the corner of his eye.

"No more jokes like that," Big Jimmy said in a deadpan tone.

"Let's see it one more time, what do you say?" Two was like a stuck record. He couldn't get his mind off it.

Since they were unable to talk him out of it, they went back to the hotel to get some sleep, leaving him curled up like an abandoned child in front of the door, where he waited for the 1:00 AM show.

Two still hadn't returned by noon the next day, so they split up to look for him in the casino and the theater. They didn't find him. When it was time to head back to the university, the three of them began grumbling, and finally decided they'd have to go back without him. Big Jimmy surmised on the trip home that Two was avoiding them because he didn't want to spend any more money.

Little Jimmy said that Two wasn't as considerate as Big Jimmy. A week later Zhu Li heard somewhere that Two had been seen hopping out of the cab of a refrigerator truck, his eyes sunken in, looking only about half human, his legs shaking so badly that his knees were knocking. Someone else said he'd seen Two in a suit, with an American woman on his arm as he stepped out of a limousine... whatever the case, anything was possible where Two was involved and eighty or ninety percent of the stories were fabricated. When all's said and done, pooling everyone's wisdom is a helluva lot better than anything I can come up with here.

45

A month later I was out strolling in the park when I spotted Two teaching Tai Chi to a bunch of American senior citizens. As always, he was wearing stone-washed jeans, his hair was shoulder length, and he had a far-off look in his eyes. According to him, he had to get up every morning at seven and rush over to the park half-dressed so he could earn enough for next semester's tuition and rent.

Chapter 5

When she spotted his flippant smiling face at the Oakland airport she had to fight to keep her feelings of disgust from surfacing as she walked up to him.

"You're cold!" He put his arm around her shoulder.

Acting as natural as possible, and as stately, she twisted free and asked as though everything was fine, "Do you have a car?"

"My little beauty, how can anyone live in the States without a car?" He put his arm around her shoulder again.

She felt like spitting in his face or slapping him, but then she thought about the man whose bed she'd shared for all those years, yet who'd never once fulfilled his responsibilities as a husband, and even though the man next to her now was little more than a thug, in the end there wasn't much difference. She brushed his arm away, as though it belonged to Two.

"Where am I staying tonight, Mr. Sheng?"

"Don't you worry your pretty head. You'll stay where I stay."

"At your home? I should have brought a gift for your wife."

"She's American. She won't care."

"What should I give you?"

"You're the best present I could ask for." He wrapped his hand around hers, which was doubled into a fist.

She shuddered and pulled her hand, free, a feeling of nausea in the pit of her stomach. But she forced it back and said coolly, "I'll give you a painting by the famous artist Shao Fei. That should be enough to express my gratitude for your help."

He smiled, embarrassed." I've reserved you a room in Motel 6."

"How much a night? Will I be able to find a job tomorrow?"

"What's the hurry. You don't need to be afraid as long as I'm around. Let's get a late-night snack. There's a place near the motel." After putting her suitcases and handbag into the car, he walked her over to a fancy bar, holding her close to him.

"What would you like to drink? Whiskey?"

"I don't drink."

"Don't any of you women from China drink?"

"Some do. I'm allergic to alcohol."

"What would you like then?"

"Apple juice."

"Too common. How about a martini?"

"No, I'd like apple juice."

"Waitress, an apple juice and a pina colada."

"You have lovely hands. A manicure and some polish would make you really sexy." He used this as an excuse to hold her hand, as a faint smell of alcohol floated over toward her. She acted calm, although she felt like a girl who'd been sold into a brothel. After flicking his hand away, she wiped her hand with the napkin, then picked up the check and went to pay it.

48

"Sit down and finish your drink," he said, grabbing her hand and looking hurt. "Show a little class." "I didn't come to sell my body," she hissed through clenched teeth.

"What are you talking about? You must be joking! Why'd you come looking for me if you don't trust me?" Anger had crept into his voice.

"I came because I didn't believe you were evil. Of course, you don't have to help if you don't want to." Although she only had twenty dollars in her purse she insisted on paying the ten-dollar bar check to give the impression there was plenty more where that came from.

"Anyone better than a wolf is a good man, anyone worse is a bad man," she said, looking him straight in the eye. His expression was not an attractive one. On their way to the motel he was the perfect gentleman, not once giving her one of his devilish looks. She used this as an excuse to put some distance between them, assuming lofty airs and ignoring his change in attitude. When they reached the motel, he handed her the key and said sternly, "Number five. Carry your own things so you won't be scared."

"I don't know the meaning of the word fear. Good night." She dragged and carried her luggage from the car to the motel room. Then, following a brief inspection of the room, including the door and windows, she dragged two easy chairs over to block the locked door, and, instead of washing up or brushing her teeth, lay down fully clothed to figure out how she was going to pay for the room. By selling some pieces of jade and handicrafts in Chinatown she'd have enough to stay for three days, during which she'd check the Chinese newspaper want ads for work.

A knock at the door. Her heart raced. She tiptoed over to the window, parted the curtains, and peeked out. In the misty moonlight she recognized the face that always smiled. Why would anyone smile like that all the time, even in the moonlight with no one looking? Her first reaction to his smile was a feeling that she was fated to be stuck

49

forever to that dirty, sticky face. Having already figured out that his bark was worse than his bite, she invited him in and sat down across from him, where she stared at his disgusting smiling face. "Let's talk," she said stiffly. "I'd like to tell you what kind of person I am, if you have the time."

"Of course I have. As soon as I saw you on the airplane I knew you were different from other people, and I fell for you on the spot..."

"That's all the more reason for you to have an understanding of my family and me. My father was a high-ranking member of the public security bureau in a certain city. He died in 1976. My mother and stepfather are both ministerial-level cadres. I came to visit my husband, but he can't support me, so I've come to you. If you help me out now, when my back's against the wall, I'll never forget it, and I'll pay you back ten-fold. Since you often do business with China, my family and I will give you all the assistance we can. But if you have other ideas and try to take advantage of my delicate situation, we'll never forgive you, and if you so much as step foot in China..." hmph! She stopped her tirade in mid-sentence and looked straight into the face that seemed to have been born with a smile and grinned menacingly.

"Boy, how you've changed. You're scary. Yesterday on the plane, the way you kept your head down I figured you'd be easy to talk to, and I wouldn't have to watch what I said. But today you're a different person..." He spread a Chinese newspaper out in front of her as a goodwill gesture. "A family in the Richmond district is looking for a nanny who can speak Mandarin. Seven fifty a month plus room and board. This one's looking for someone to take care of an old lady, nine hundred a month plus room and board. But they'll only take someone with a social security card who knows how to drive and can speak English... I already phoned them. You can go over tomorrow."

As she looked down at the newspaper, which was marked up with notes of the phone conversations, gratitude welled up in her

50

heart, that plus a rush of pity for this poor little man who always had sex on his mind but lacked the courage to match his desires. She'd later have no recollection of how much she talked that night and for how long, but she remembered bringing all her skills into play to convince him that she and her family had plenty of clout in China. She bragged of everything under the sun, short of claiming Mao Zedong and Deng Xiaoping as uncles, suppressing her natural timidity to indulge in one exaggeration after another. Fortunately, he was an insignificant businessman who wanted only to take advantage of her as a woman, but lacked the skills to get her into bed. Whether it was because she had frightened him off or because, like insignificant businessmen everywhere, he never forgot his times tables, she didn't know, but as he was leaving the motel he said with somewhat sarcastic respect, "You people from China all come equipped with your theories. Is that what the Cultural Revolution taught you? I'll pick you up and take you over tomorrow."

"Thank you." Her gaze, now gentle, lit on the second button of his shirt; her long eyelashes fluttered slightly as a glinting watery film covered her eyes. This change in her eyes gave him renewed confidence as his gaze swept across her face.

"Can I have a hug? It's an American custom," he stammered pitifully as he was leaving. Like someone handing small change to a beggar, she allowed herself to be squeezed before saying goodbye and nearly pushing him out the door, which she locked behind him. Then she flopped down on the bed, covered her head with the pillow, and lay there till dawn without closing her eyes. The next day he neither took her to see anyone nor so much as phoned. Although that made her feel a bit anxious, it wasn't unexpected. A man like that would never help a woman he couldn't take to bed. As an economy measure, all she ate that day were an apple and half a piece of cake, both leftovers from her flight. She made a couple of phone calls, but the responses were short and simple: "Come see us, and bring your ID card." Come see us? A strange place, with no friends, no English, and no car — easier said than done. Bringing all her resources to bear, she managed to locate the two houses, but left disappointed from each. One family wouldn't hire her because she had no social

51

security card, didn't know how to drive, and couldn't speak English. The other gave no reasons, just sent her away. Only one avenue left: the occupation she despised more than any other — a nanny. She returned to the motel, took ten tiny pills for a throat infection, and lay down on the bed, where she was struck by a sudden longing to go home to China. It was a powerful, miserable feeling. The thousand dollars for the air ticket and all she'd spent for luggage and clothes had nearly wiped her out, and if she went back empty-handed she couldn't set up a decent home if she worked like a slave for ten years. All those people who left no stone unturned to get out somehow, and many more who were in a constant state of anxiety in order to come up with enough bucks to apply.

In a tiny, damp two-room house she and her co-worker, Nine-Headed Bird were to meet a middle-aged policewoman, their Goddess of Mercy. Before she entered the room Nine-Headed Bird told her, "Don't say a word. Just take out that painting by Shao Fei and let her take the lead. You can't lose." She'd barely sat down when Nine-Headed Bird hastily hung Shao Fei's painting on the gray wall and bragged about how many international exhibits the artist had had and how her paintings sold for hundreds of dollars. The policewoman smiled warmly as she took the painting down, rolled it up, and laid it down beside Shan Naiwo. "It's lovely," she said, "but since I'm working on your passport I can't take it. After you leave, we'll be friends. And if you want to bring me back a VCR, I won't say no." The word "leave" had such a wonderful ring to it that Shan Naiwo's anxieties dissolved as the policewoman returned the painting to her. A rumor was going around that the American Consulate would no longer be issuing F-2 visas after October first. It was a terrifying thought, and she knew she had to get her passport in a hurry. Nine-Headed Bird understood perfectly what was going through both women's minds: She wanted to make a gift of the painting, but couldn't force it upon the policewoman, while the policewoman wanted the painting, but didn't dare say so outright. So she took a roundabout course of action. "We're old friends," she said, "changing her tone, and I'd never ask you to knowingly break the law. I asked the artist herself to give you this painting, but if you

52

think it might cause trouble, I'll take it back and ask Shao Fei to inscribe it for you."

"No!" The policewoman instinctively placed her hand on the rolled-up painting. "Experts say that an inscription lowers a painting's value! The black-market exchange rate is 7.50 RMB to a dollar. My son's going to register for the TOEFL next month, and they say the registration fee is up to $56. You know I don't have any family overseas to send us money and we don't dare use the black market..."

Nine-Headed Bird knew exactly what she meant. In a jocular tone she articulated, without actually using the words, what the policewoman was getting at. "As I see it, it would be a shame to hang a painting like this on some dark old wall. Why not let Shan Naiwo sell the painting for what she can get, and help your son out by giving him enough to take the test a couple of times."

None of the three women could say what was on their minds, but Nine-Headed Bird had made it sound as though Shan Naiwo was getting the better deal. Since she was in such desperate need of a passport, she agreed, taking a hundred dollars out of her purse and laying it on the table. "This painting's worth at least two hundred," she said softly in the tone of someone paying off a debt. "I'll bring another hundred over tomorrow." Worried that the policewoman might have second thoughts, she said a hasty goodbye and dragged Nine-Headed Bird out the door, but the policewoman stopped her, took a look around, and whispered conspiratorially, "Your passport will be ready the day after tomorrow. Line up like everybody else and pretend you don't know me. Forget the other hundred."

Shan Naiwo's overwhelming gratitude seemed to stick in her throat. She nodded a dozen times or so, accompanied by some indistinct mumbling, before taking Nine-Headed Bird's hand and walking quickly down the lane. "You really are a nine-headed bird!" she said. Her friend laid an index finger across Shan Naiwo's mouth, forming the character for China, and said softly, "Keeping your mouth shut is what China's all about."

"Let's celebrate. The Emerald China Restaurant. My treat."

"No, let me. My last chance to dote on you. After you get to the States you'll be waiting tables, washing dishes, and cleaning toilets, always taking care of other people."

That took the edge off Shan Naiwo's enthusiasm. Like the dying rays of a setting sun, in a final orgy of beauty before being swallowed up in the west, her momentary excitement soon vanished.

Another morning. Nine-Headed Bird woke her up. "It's true, the American Consulate is going to stop issuing F-2 visas on October 1st!"

"That's just a rumor," she said to mask her panic heart.

"Why not go over and get your visa?"

"I still don't have a formal letter from my husband."

"That bastard! That goddamned Two! What's he up to? Who ever heard of someone not wanting to be together with his wife?"

"He says he can't support me. Maybe he's planning on returning. Or maybe he doesn't want me to come so soon."

"So *soon*? In the West, living apart for two years is the same as seeking a divorce. Enough of that nonsense. Get me one of his letters and a piece of thin stationery."

"What for?"

"We'll forge a letter by tracing his handwriting."

"You really are a Nine-Headed Bird! Whatever it, you can do it!"

"First find the word 'dear.'"

"There isn't one. He only uses that with his mother. Never with me."

"Okay, then we'll use the word 'Little,' and add your name, Naiwo. That's nice and intimate, isn't it? Okay. Now find the words 'after you get here,' 'housing,' and 'financial problem.' Fine, now I add the word 'no' to 'financial problem.' Find something like 'I hope to see you soon.'"

"How about this: 'I hope you'll send me the books I wanted soon.'"

"Here, this is good: 'When you see Xie Er tell him to hurry up and return my book.'"

"Everything we need is in those two sentences."

"Last but not least, find a '!' for me."

"He never uses exclamation marks."

"No problem, that one I can handle. There, perfect!"

"There's another problem. My financial guarantee is a bank affidavit without my name or anything else."

"I'll fill it in for you. Borrow a typewriter. But I've never seen a financial guarantee form, so I'm not sure what to write."

"It's no laughing matter, since I only have one copy. If we screw it up, I've had it."

"It's already six o'clock, so we can't waste time. Today's the 30th."

"To hell with it, I'm too tired to worry about it."

"You can't give up now. Not before the last step of your Long March, not before the last of your seventy-two kowtows. Come on, let's go to the International Hotel. The place is crawling with foreigners. We'll ask one of them. We can take the typewriter along and fill out the form there." Five minutes later they had freshened up, including some lipstick for effect.

Once her papers were in order she went to the Consulate Section of the American Embassy at 17 North Xiushui Street. Nine-Headed Bird took her hand and gave final instructions: "Don't act humble or haughty. Just be natural. When they ask if you plan to stay in the States, say no, that life's too good in China. If it's a woman, wipe off your lipstick. Everybody says they hate attractive women..." Another long, restive, sun-drenched line. She turned and looked back at Nine-Headed Bird, who was standing on the other side of the green metal fence looking blankly at her, like someone visiting a loved one in prison or saying goodbye. As her eyes misted up, Shan Naiwo lowered her head. Finally, after standing in line for a long time, she was ushered into a room. It was so quiet you could hear a pin drop. On the other side of a screen a line of people, old and young, male and female, sat next to a wall beyond a chain barrier. It looked like the Devil's Gate or the Bridge of Hell. Their pale faces were filled with an anxiety they were trying hard to mask as they waited silently for their names to be called.

A young man behind her gently tugged her sleeve and pointed out the window, where she saw Nine-Headed Bird frantically signaling to her. She ran over to the barricade, where she got the latest news: "If they ask how much you make a month, tell them 300 RMB. That's more or less the truth, if you add your earnings from your performances and your foreign currency. Five people just came out who were refused F-2 visas. But don't worry, they have a quota, so they can't turn everyone down. Besides, your financial guarantee is rock-solid." No longer the normally clever, calm Nine-Headed Bird, she seemed more anxious than her friend, who walked back to the visa section to silently await the moment of truth.

56

"Wo B. Dan." A soft male voice with a heavy foreign accent called out her name, mispronouncing her surname and misreading the character 'nai' (   ) as the initial B.

Her heart, under so much pressure, seemed to crash to the ground and explode, like a falling light bulb. She looked up and wafted behind the curtain, every movement followed by countless pairs of eyes. It took less than five minutes. The handsomely bearded Mr. Lake had nodded amiably and said, "I just love your Chinese folk dances. I hope when you get to America you'll have a chance to meet some of our dancers." She was so tense, so excited, and she found this crummy little man unbearable. She felt like throwing up. Her head seemed about to explode from the pressure. Giving him the most charming smile she could manage, she walked out through the prison-door of a gate.

"Did you get it?"

"J-2 or F-1?"

"What did they ask you? What did you tell them?"

The crowd outside the gate rushed up to her with questions.

Without stopping to answer them, she ran over to Nine-Headed Bird, who was still standing beyond the green metal barricade like a wooden decoy; she rested her head on Nine-Headed Bird's shoulder, Nine-Headed Bird held her band. Neither of them said a word as they walked over to where they'd parked their bikes.

"Nine-Headed Bird, Nine-Headed Bird, for your sake, I can't turn and run at the first sign of trouble!" she exclaimed as she climbed out of bed and walked over to the mirror. She was repulsed by the sallow reflection, the same way she had been repulsed by that pair of bewitching 'phoenix' eyes. Later that night she had a terrible headache and a high fever, and didn't know how she could possibly make it to dawn. After trying, unsuccessfully, to get up several times, she slept fitfully till morning.

Mr. Sheng's frantic knocking finally forced her out of bed.

"I'm sorry, I had to take my son to the hospital with a fever, and my wife wouldn't let me leave his side. How are you doing?"

"I'm okay."

"Did you go see them? What happened?" Apparently he'd forgotten his promises.

"Nothing suitable." She was calm and detached.

"I took care of your motel bill. Are you free today?"

"Yes. I ran a fever last night. Probably catching cold..."

Without waiting for her to finish, he said, "I'm really swamped at the office today. Stuff that should have been shipped has been piling up over the past few days. Come give me a hand. Since it's too expensive to live in a motel, work for me for a few days and you can stay at my mother's house."

"Okay." She agreed even though she had a splitting headache and ached all over. If a businessman pays for three nights in a motel without demanding your favors in return, you're obligated to pay him back somehow. So she spent the next two days in his dark, dank, mildewy warehouse cleaning dirty old gears and moving heavy crates, going to work early and coming home late, allowing herself only a few minutes at noon for a quick sandwich and a glass of milk. Her body ached, and she nearly collapsed several times, but her mind was at peace.

Chapter 6

All the Chinese newspapers carried the same story about a certain couple from the mainland, both overseas students, who sought political asylum on New Year's Day, fearing the worst from the Communist government because she was pregnant with her second child. An INS source said the case was so special that asylum would likely be granted.

On the same day the *New York Times* printed a story about a Chinese overseas student who had walked from San Francisco to Alaska, a trip that took him forty days. When a reporter asked the longhaired, gaunt student, who was wearing stone-washed jeans, why he had done it, he had narrowed his eyes, which looked like those of classical Chinese beauty, and smiled without answering. The reporter then asked if it was true that he planned to spend his summer vacation walking across Canada; once again he smiled but said nothing.

Chapter 7

For Americans the weekend is a brief holiday, particularly for the young. The five preceding days of work all seem to be a prelude to the last two: plans for the weekend — what to do, how to do it, how to make it different and exciting — begin on Monday morning. For most Chinese students in America the weekend takes on different patterns: with the exception of working in a Chinese restaurant, studying, writing papers, grocery shopping for the week, and enjoying a good meal, the most attractive prospects involve going to yard sales. If you're lucky you can pick up a decent suit for fifty cents, or for as little as a dollar you can buy a typewriter, a tape recorder, a TV set, or some other home appliance. In other words, for next to nothing you can buy some good stuff and enjoy the thrill of driving a hard bargain. Even I'm hooked, like a drug addict. Here in Salt Lake City, a town known for its Mormons, once the winter has passed, I spend as much time as I can at yard sales, which fit the description of one of Mao Zedong's lines of poetry: No scenery compares to this.

Early one weekend morning Big Jimmy drove Two and me, classified ads in hand, for a trip around town. Our first stop was a church where damaged goods were being sold at incredibly low prices. Large shopping bags filled with clothing were going for two dollars and shoes in vastly varying condition for fifty cents a pair. Two spent two dollars on four pairs of quite usable slip-on shoes, but Big Jimmy reminded him that he was wasting his money no matter how cheap they were. But Two just narrowed his 'phoenix' eyes and said he could use them. Big Jimmy took a different approach, buying only inexpensive and very unusual items, like a skeleton, an old-fashioned telephone, a pair of binoculars, car tires, a wall decoration, Chinese and Japanese paintings...a big pile of stuff. All right, I thought, now Big Jimmy has joined the overseas Chinese student middle class: in addition to having enough to eat and wear and always looking for bargains, he'd begun paying attention to aesthetics! We made a few more stops, filling the car with more and more stuff, all of it Big Jimmy's, except for a canteen and a sleeping bag that Two had bought. Spread out on the lawn at one home were a mere nineteen items. Big Jimmy surprised us by buying it all for ten dollars. Unusual, to say the least. "Give me a hand," he said to Two. "Help me take the stuff out of the car." Then, like a magician, he produced a cloth bag and emptied its contents out on the ground. There were a dozen or more boxes of balms and ointments, which he separated into piles, then began making his sales pitch to passersby. "Good morning miss. This is China's famous Wan Jin Oil, a unique medicinal balm. It works on headaches, fevers, and insect bites, and can remove facial wrinkles."

A woman who looked like a Mexican said, "If it can do all that, how much does it cost?"

"It's supposed to sell for ten dollars a bottle," Big Jimmy answered quickly, "but for a someone as lovely as you I'll take two."

Two tittered and shoved him lightly in the chest. "You're a wizard," he said in Chinese.

Big Jimmy was pleased. "I brought too much with me when I came. It doesn't do me any good." He turned and announced to a black woman, "China's unique healing balm. A secret formula from the imperial court. Enriches the blood and enhances the kidneys. Cures impotence and premature ejaculation."

"The blacks are as strong as oxen," I said softly. "They don't need their kidneys enhanced."

The quick-witted Big Jimmy quickly changed his tune. "Another unique function is that it reduces the dark pigment in skin cells..." he lowered his voice and said to Two, "Look, here come a couple of old ladies. Tell them it's good for aches, pains, and dizzy spells."

Familiar with the American fear of growing old, Two said, "Restores the energy level, better than the Fountain of Youth..." he stopped in mid-sentence and said to Big Jimmy in Chinese, You know it's illegal to hawk medicine in the States.

Big Jimmy had an answer. "Tell them it's a sort of cosmetic." "Good morning, Madam, a nice jacket, isn't it. Try it on, I'm sure you'll love it." He helped her stuff her fat figure into the jacket.

"Oh, it's too small," the enormous woman muttered as she let him put it on her.

"Ah, a smaller jacket gives you that special look!" Big Jimmy flattered her as he helped her button it up. She gave him a dollar and walked off in her new jacket. "Is that how you take care of your wife at home?" Two asked.

Big Jimmy laughed. "She takes care of me... oh, so you're here, too. Take whatever you like," he said to Zhu Li and another Chinese girl from her department.

After several refusals, Zhu Li tossed down fifty cents and picked up a toaster. That didn't please him. "Forget it," he said forcefully, "I don't want your money."

After they'd walked off, Zhu Li said to her friend. "That one will do whatever he has to do to stay."

"What's that?" the other girl said teasingly. "Are you jealous because he won't have anything to do with you now that his wife's here?"

"It takes more than something like that to bother me."

"I'm glad to see that somebody's broken the spell men have on us. It's a pity that so many of us overseas students get together with men, even marry them, for reasons other than love."

"Romance is the sort of poetry you write after a big dinner. We're not like you government-sponsored students, for whom the

64

Chinese people tighten their belts to give you seven hundred a month."

"I'd be happy to trade my seven hundred for your F-1 visa. You can stay, but we have to go back. Say, didn't you get a research assistantship for next year?"

"They gave it to someone else."

"Why?"

"Somehow my advisor found out that I hadn't done any research in that field in China and that the recommendation letters were phony... he gave the assistantship to Big Jimmy."

"Americans hate lying."

"I scored less than 550 on my TOEFL, and to get into school, he..."

"Ah, so that's it."

"We're both wolves that have come in from the wilderness. There's a phone booth in front of that ice-cream shop. Wait here for me."

"I'll go with you. Where do you want to cross?"

"No, you stay here. I have some intimate things to say to a certain man."

"Ha ha, so you can't break the spell of men, after all."

"Ha ha, when I'm finished I'll buy you an ice cream."

She returned a few minutes later with two chocolate ice-cream cones, licking one as she signaled her mend to come along with her.

Big Jimmy's business was booming, and it caught the attention of a passing police car, which pulled up and stopped in front of his yard sale. "Have you registered with City Hall?" one of the policemen asked politely.

Given a momentary fright, Big Jimmy just stood there with his mouth open, stuck for an answer.

"You need permission to hold a yard sale," the policeman said, "or you could be fined a hundred dollars."

Big Jimmy was shaking in his boots, his fists were clenched. He gave Two a helpless look.

Two narrowed his bewitching 'phoenix' eyes and thought for a moment. "I know, go ask that last place if they had permission."

Big Jimmy turned and ran back to the house with the big lawn and quickly returned with a yellow slip of paper. He strode confidently up to the policeman and read in a loud voice, "Signed by Alice. Registration number 423!"

The policemen shrugged their shoulders, one of them grumbling, "It's a damned lie" and left.

On the surface, Big Jimmy appeared perfectly calm, but the incident had nearly scared him out of his wits. When the policemen were gone, he grabbed Two's hand and stood there without saying a word.

Chapter 8

Two stepped on the gas and shoved the pickup into first, but it just shuddered, unable to climb the hill. Abandoning the truck, he walked up the bill to take a look around; except for a pile of stones among the dense shrubbery on a hill shaped like a volcano, he saw no number 66. So he wafted back down the hill, took the classified section of the newspaper out of the pickup, and checked the street sign to make sure he was right. He was. But just as he was about to leave he remembered passing a nice home with a large garden and a mailbox with the number 65. Number 66 must be around here somewhere. That's strange. Just then a black man with a scraggly beard appeared as though he'd fallen out of the sky. With friendly concern he asked, "You looking for number 66, sir?"

"Yeah. Where is it?"

"Over there," the black man pointed uphill with his hairy chin.

Suddenly getting the picture, Two turned and ran back up the hill, where he carefully studied the volcano-like pile of stones and discovered what appeared to be a door at the southern edge. He pressed a stone whose color was slightly different than the others, and, sure enough, heard the faint sound of a bell from inside. He pressed it again and waited. Before long, he heard someone say "So, you forgot your key again, Pig brain," followed by the sound of banging on the wall, as the stone gate opened a crack. Two was confronted by a skeletal, white face and a cold gleam of light that gave him a momentary fright, then a crumpled little body in a glistening chrome wheelchair. Two took a step backward. The old man glared menacingly at him. "What do you want? How did you find this place?"

Two took another step backward and pointed to the classified ad. "Didn't you advertise for help?"

The old man reached a trembling, tiny, bony hand through the crack and took the newspaper, then shakily put on a pair of reading glasses. "Henry, you pig!" he swore. "You're supposed to give notice before you quit, you damned turtle, you stupid pig brain. Well, I didn't give him this week's wages..." the old man spun his wheelchair around with difficulty, seemingly having forgotten all about Two, who squeezed through the crack in the wall and found himself in a bright, spacious living room. He realized that the concave hilltop was in fact a huge overhead skylight. The walls around him were dotted with tiny drain holes for the water. Two arcing wheelchair tracks ran beside the wall, one leading down to the basement, the other running up to a large stone terrace with what seemed to be a huge enclosed bookcase, so ancient it looked like a bronze artifact right out of the ground. Even on his tiptoes, Two couldn't see what was inside. Meanwhile, the old man was straining to wheel himself up the track, but made little progress before rolling back down to the living room floor and banging into one of the walls. "Hey, pig, are you blind?" the old man screamed at Two.

Two smiled, then wheeled the old man up to the terrace, where he was waved away. Once Two was back on ground level, the old man opened the narrow doors of the bookcase and wheeled himself inside, leaving silence behind. Two walked over and sat down on a sofa, where he spotted a pink slip of paper on the armrest: Clean sofa covers every other week. He decided to stick it up on the refrigerator door so he wouldn't forget, but there was another slip there already: One meal a day. Place tray next to door on terrace. Bottle of mineral water, two slices of black bread, turkey, yogurt, lettuce. Altogether, Two found a dozen or so of the pink reminders, which told him everything he needed to know except where he was to sleep and how many hours he was expected to work each day. Trying to find a bed was like walking into minefield. He stepped very gingerly down the ramp to the basement, but the passage was so dark he couldn't see his hand in front of his face, even though it was the middle of the day, and his eyes were suddenly superfluous. He felt the walls with his hands, up one side and down the other, without finding a door. Then he tried again, and this time his hand brushed up against a light switch on the wall, which he tried a few times, but with no results. Time to give up. He went back into the living room, where he lay down on the sofa and took a nap. When he woke up he went to the refrigerator to make the old man's lunch in accordance with instructions on the slip of paper. After making something for himself first, he took the old man's tray up to the terrace at the specified time. He knocked on the snugly closed doors, but didn't hear a sound from inside. With a nagging suspicion that the old guy might already have passed on to a better world, he knocked again, twice.

"I know, pig! Didn't that pig Henry tell you to put it down next to the door? Get lost!" The old man's curses emerged from behind the narrow doors, which remained closed. The chastened but befuddled Two walked back down to the living room, not even turning to look when he heard the narrow doors being opened, and lay down on the sofa, where he gradually fell asleep. Huh, huh? He awoke with a start to the loud crashing of plates and trays, and snapped his eyes open just in time to see a four-wheeled bamboo hamper filled to the top with dirty dishes, dirty clothes, and an assortment of trash and garbage careen down the sloping track, bang into the wall, and roll over up next to him. He dug out the printed reminder for his Wednesday duties, which required three slips of paper: 1. Put dirty laundry into washing machine, clean the living room, the two ramps, and the skylight — use the hanging ladder. 2. Buy groceries for the week... the third slip said to go down the hill to pick up some mineral water. For the next four hours Two worked like a madman, working up quite a sweat, but only managed to clean the skylight and the two ramps. He stopped, since it was already six o'clock, picked up two plastic containers, and rushed outside, not giving a thought to the laundry, which had long since been washed. But when he got to the bottom of the hill he realized he'd forgotten to bring the slip of paper that told him where he was to pick up the mineral water. As he turned to walk back, the bearded black man, who was holding two containers of mineral water in his hands, blocked his way. "How's everything going?" he asked happily. "You're twenty minutes late. You're supposed to be here, not leave, at six."

"Sorry I made you wait, Sir. I'll be on time from now on." Recalling all the work that awaited him at home, Two didn't feel like chatting with the black man, so he picked up the containers and started up the hill.

"Don't forget to bring the water coupon along next Wednesday," the black man shouted at Two's retreating back. "In the cupboard."

Two just grunted a reply, not daring to stop. When he walked into the living room, the old man was on the terrace, a hateful glare on his white skeletal face. "What time do I take my bath?" he shouted apoplectically. "What time do I take my bath? Didn't that pig Henry tell you!"

Two dug out the dozen or so pink reminders and searched through them. Sure enough, the ninth slip informed him that the old man took his bath at half past six. He put down the containers of mineral water and started up the ramp with the old man's curses raining down on him from the terrace, then wheeled him down the ramp. But he'd no sooner pushed him into the bathroom than he was waved out the door, which was slammed in his face. Wondering how the old guy got undressed and bathed himself in the wheelchair, Two got down on his hands and knees and pressed his ear up to the door to figure out what was going on inside. First came the sound of water faucets being tuned on, followed by many, contented, gloriously happy moans. Two couldn't keep from giggling out loud, which brought an immediate cessation of sounds from inside. "Get the hell away from there!" The shout ripped through the cracks of the door. "Get the hell away from there!" Two forced back his giggles and walked in place as though he were leaving. Then he got back down on his hands and knees to listen some more. The old man started moaning again. About a half hour later, Two picked out some clean clothes, using a pink reminder as a guide, and put them in the hamper beside the bathroom door, then meekly retreated to the sofa to await the old man's next command. The wheelchair rolled out of the bathroom. The old man's skeletal face had undergone a metamorphosis: his cheeks were rosy, the stiffness had vanished, and

70

his skin looked soft and touchable. Two rushed over and wheeled him up the ramp to the terrace. With the corners of his eyes turned up in a smile, the old man waved one of his white, bony hands and said warmly, "You start tomorrow, a hundred and fifty a week. Let's sign an agreement." He pulled out three copies of an agreement prepared ahead of time, and signed them, then handed them to Two, who very carefully read the agreement. "There's a mistake here. Today's the sixth."

"No mistake," the old man said, his shoulders slumped over in the wheelchair. "Tomorrow's the seventh."

"What about today?"

The old man's expression changed, as the redness was swallowed up by white. "Pig, I never said I was going to hire you today! I have no legal responsibility without a signed agreement. If you want to work for nothing that's all right with me. Why should I pay you? All people are pigs. Their brains don't work so good."

"You're forgetting about the foxes," Two said in a low voice, like an old man reading a story to his grandson.

"You're not mad? Your clothes are soaked, you're beat to your socks, I've been yelling at you and I'm not going to pay you, and you're not mad?" The old man was trying to agitate Two.

Two looked at him as though he were a toy in his son's hand. "You want to see me get mad?"

"Even when you're wrong you're apathetic? You Chinese are all so apathetic... oh, I'm sorry, maybe you're Japanese."

Two's expression didn't change as he looked at the old man, except a bit more white showed in his eyes, as the dark irises seemed to shrink.

"Are you willing to stay on even if I don't pay you for today?"

71

"You're damned right!" Two bellowed, a scary, savage quake in his throat.

The old man kept calm, but his face was as rigid as an inert skull. A moment passed, and he looked up at Two, timidly, like a child that's lost its mother, his mouth, so given to ridicule and cursing, tightly shut. Two pointed to the old man's forehead, as though he were training a household pet, and said, "You will stop yelling at me as a release for your own mental hang-ups and forget about exercising that body of yours, which is beyond any need for exercise. If you ever yell at me again I'll sue you for physical and mental anguish."

The old man's rock-hard expression melted like a river in spring. He was changing again. Finally a child-like smile spread across his face and he complimented Two on wising up.

Two's 'phoenix' eyes also recaptured their bewitching quality. "The forest's so big," he said with a sigh, "it's home to all kinds of birds."

The old man's vital signs were back to normal. "Are you from China?" he asked spiritedly. "Do you know how to do *qigong* breathing exercises? How about Tai Chi?"

Two scrutinized the shriveled old body in the wheelchair, his 'phoenix' eyes arching upward as he looked the old man up and down. "They won't do you any good, I'm afraid, he said teasingly."

The old man threw his head back and laughed, like a braying donkey. You could hear the phlegm rattling around in his throat: "Energy comes from Heaven and the Universe, trust and sincerity determine skills... shame on you. Are you really from ancient China?"

Two suddenly saw the old man in a different light, but before he could mull over what he'd just said, a command rang in his ears: "Wheel me upstairs, and be quick about it!" Without saying a word,

72

Two wheeled him up to the terrace, keeping his eyes averted, as expected, and turned to walk downstairs. He'd only taken a few steps before the narrow doors opened and quickly closed, sending a breath of cold air sweeping past him and causing his heart to throb with fear. He smoothed down the hair that had stood on end and rushed downstairs, where he threw himself down on the sofa and promptly fell into a deep sleep. But he hadn't been sleeping long when he awoke with a fright, then fell back to sleep, then woke up again, over and over, at least ten times that night, until he finally fell asleep and stayed asleep sometime before dawn, snoring loudly. This time Two awoke to warm rays of the morning sun streaming in through the skylight. After wiping his sweaty face, he glanced at his watch, and jumped to his feet. He was wide awake. Springing into action, he prepared the old man's lunch, not even taking time out to feed himself, and ran with it up to the terrace. He was surprised to find one of the narrow doors open and the wheelchair stuck in the opening. The old man's bone-white face was lying up against the back of the chair, an oxygen bag the size of a pillow resting in his lap, its gray tubes stuck up his nostrils like roundworms. Just as Two walked up to him, the old man stirred, straining to wave the hand that had been holding the oxygen bag. Two froze on the spot, not daring to take another step. He flipped through the pink reminders and asked timidly: "Shall I take you to the hospital?" "No." "Should I call for a doctor?" "No." "Should I call your sons?" "No." As Two looked at the old man's bloodless lips his legs turned rubbery and he sat down on the floor in front of the doors, from where he watched the old man's illness proceed. Before long the old man's nostrils twitched and his eyes rolled up in his head. Two jumped to his feet and nearly flew downstairs to call for an ambulance and the old man's sons. The ambulance stand warmly agreed to send someone over at once. His sons, on the other hand, were decidedly cool. "Has Henry been replaced?" one of them asked. "It's the same old problem. A little oxygen and he'll be fine." The other said, "He'd probably be okay by the time I got off the plane. And if he was he sure wouldn't want to see me. You're new at this. Henry wouldn't get all upset like this." Two was completely mystified when he hung up the phone; he felt like he was floating in the air like a cloud, as though the old man and everything around him were totally beyond his comprehension. When his gaze returned to the old man, it was as though they were in different worlds. He'd just done what anybody else would do in similar circumstances, but it looked as though father and sons were so antagonistic that his facilitating efforts were wasted. The wail of an ambulance siren split the air, startling Two, who rushed downstairs to open the door and admit four hulking men carrying lifesaving equipment. "Where is he?" one of them asked Two, who led them up to the terrace. But the doors were closed, and from the other side came a weak voice: "Get them out of here, right now! I said I wouldn't see a doctor... since you called them, pay them and tell them to leave..."

Two seemed to be catching on, although nothing was as clear as it should have been. Swallowing the old man's abuse, he obeyed his command like a mechanical man, writing out a check and sending the men packing. From that day on Two followed the pink reminders to the letter, either spending his days running around or sitting there twiddling his thumbs or listening to the old man rant and rave and give him hell or screaming at the old man so viciously he didn't dare so much as look at Two for days on end. They lived together in relative peace; sometimes they actually hit it off pretty well. At the beginning of the third week Two forgot his place and burst in on the old man while he was taking his bath. He stared at the skinny fossil-like legs as though his eyes were glued to them. Outraged, the old man sprayed him in the face with water. His eyes stinging and face burning, the wide-eyed Two walked up to the old man, obsessed with the notion of touching those legs that were truly skin and bones and looked as though they'd been buffeted by the elements for at least a century. He wanted to know what an icy fossil felt like first-hand. He also wanted to hear what it sounded like if you hit them with something hard. Straining to pull the shower nozzle off the wall, the old man pinched the rubber hose so that the water hit Two's eyes with full, knife-like force. The pain was so great Two wrapped his arms around his head and lit out of there, collapsing onto the sofa and hanging his head. It was a long time before he tried opening his eyes. Scorching rays of sunlight burned their way through the skylight the following morning, filling the living room with golden red light. Two opened his eyes very tentatively, very slowly; it wasn't as bad as he'd feared. But he continued lying on the sofa, barely moving, a lingering fear in his heart. He let his sleepy gaze roam the walls and slowly work its way up to the doors on the terrace, his nervousness increasing by the second; he could hear the sound of his own heart and his breathing more clearly than at any other time in his life. He swung his legs over the side and sat there as though in a trance, forcing himself not to look at anything, or think of anything, driving out the nervousness and excitement of a man about to go into battle, which had come upon him so suddenly.

After preparing lunch on schedule, he walked gingerly up to the terrace, not making a sound. As though they had a mind of their own, the doors flew open the moment he stood in front of them. The old man took the tray without even looking at Two and closed the doors. Although Two kept his eyes averted from the old man and the scene behind the doors, he felt a cold blast of air emerge from the cracks in the doors and brush by him. Once again he smoothed down his hair and rushed back to the living room to sit blankly on the sofa. Gradually he came to realize that he was waiting for something, a sensation that grew more and more urgent. Was he waiting for the hamper filled with dirty dishes and laundry to come careering down the ramp? Was he waiting to hear the old man's braying laugh or curses? Was he waiting for night to fall? But nothing happened, and nothing seemed clear-cut. As he began to grow fidgety, a sense of terror like that experienced by a sneak thief, began to squirm in his heart.

Late night, not a sound anywhere. Two's lips were dry and chapped, his gums seemed blistered. He lay for a while, sat for a while, got up and felt his way along the walls, went to the refrigerator for a soft drink. His heart froze when he accidentally knocked a book of matches to the floor, but that gave him an idea. Strictly speaking, this thought had lain dormant in the dark depths of his heart for a long time, and only now entered his consciousness. He pressed his ear up to the wall that supported the terrace. No sound, no movement. He walked down the ramp to the basement. The passage was so dark he felt like an eyeless creature. When his face bumped up against a metal door, although his nose smarted from the collision,

75

the odor of cold, rusty metal excited him. He lit a match and looked around: he was standing at the end of a narrow passage. The battered metal door looked just like the bookcase on the terrace, a bronze artifact right out of the ground. He pried at the door with a pocketknife until the door opened. The musty odor inside the room made him reel backwards a couple of steps. Driven by impatience, he took a deep breath and wafted into the little room, where he struck another match, the dim light revealing a red carpet with holes here and there where it had been gnawed by rats and insects. A bunch of racks holding paintings were piled up chaotically against the walls. Two looked around for some sort of light, but the room was virtually empty. The paintings aroused his curiosity, but he knew he could only keep his matches lit for about thirty seconds, so he took them out by feeling around in the dark and stacked them against the walls, then sat in the middle of the room and looked at them in the flickering light of his matches, one after another. Allowing for those he had stood up backwards, all the paintings were of skinny, diseased legs on which the skin lay so slack there seemed to be no trace of muscles beneath it, like fossils that had been weathered over a century or longer. Some glinted like bone-white jade, others were pale and lifeless; on some the white revealed a tinge of blue, on others a scaly gleam dotted an expanse of dark purple... Two lowered his eyes, feeling as though he were being penned in and dominated by piles of white bones, as though the old man had grown hundreds of fossilized legs that were pressing down on his chest all at the same time. He was having trouble breathing, his heart was racing, he felt hot and feverish. He ran out of the room before he'd used up all his matches, and bumped into the wheelchair. He screamed, but the sound was so precipitous, so shrill that it stuck in his throat and wouldn't come out; all he managed was the gurgle of a sick dog. Somehow he skirted or climbed over the wheelchair in the dark back to the safety of the living room, where he flicked on all the lights. Like a mouse in the clutches of a cat, he cast a frightened look at the open door of the basement, but stood there frozen to the spot, as the wheelchair glided into the light. The old man's face was flushed and shiny, as though he'd been drinking or had just emerged from a bath. With a grin on his face, he moved slowly toward Two, who retreated until his back was up against the stone door. Reaching behind him,

76

he opened the door and fled down the hill. When he was safely in the woods, surrounded by darkness, he breathed a sigh of relief and curled up on the exposed roots of a tall tree. The night wind licked him like the cold, wet tongue of a dog. He shivered, his teeth chattered. Over the next hour he kept shifting his sitting position and kept planning how he'd go back in the morning to see exactly what was going on back there, pick up his belongings, and demand his wages for three weeks. By then his buttocks were numb, like a slab of frozen meat, and emitted blasts of cold air. He didn't think he could make it till dawn, but at the same time he didn't feel like he ought to leave the old man alone until the sun was out. He made it through another hour, gritting his teeth without resolving his contradiction. Then just before dawn he had the hazy sense of the fine line between life and death; if he held on for one more second he'd be all right, but if fear took over, all was lost. He had no idea what happened after that, but sometime after sunrise he was discovered curled up like a sick dog at the base of the tree, his eyes glazed over like a man at death's door. According to what people said, the old man died and Two was tried in court, but found innocent of any wrongdoing. Later on they said that the old man had assumed that Two was trying to steal his priceless treasures... his lifework. That was why he'd driven Two out of his house. Still later on I ran into Two at the University of Utah, and when I put the question to him, he looked at me as though I were relating a fairy-tale and said, "Really?"

Chapter 9

Not a bad family. From Taiwan. The man, Mr. Li, was a bookish, intelligent fellow who hardly ever spoke. His wife ran a medical clinic and helped him in her spare time with real estate; her status and position kept her natural instincts in check. Genteel and sophisticated, the impression she made on Shan Naiwo was of a cultivated, graceful woman.

"It's a shame that someone like you has to work as a housekeeper, but we know how difficult it is for you self-supporting students from China. To get by in the States you have to put up with all sorts of unpleasant things, but work is only a means to an end. Keep that in mind, and you'll be all right. I came twenty years ago with fifty dollars in my pocket..."

I'll do my best, was all Shan Naiwo said.

Mrs. Li gently spelled out her duties: "I trust you. We don't go in for fancy food, and will eat whatever you make. Breakfast is casual and simple, and the only requirement for lunch is that it be nutritious for the children. Dinner's the crucial meal — No meat dishes and two vegetable, with a nice soup. We have two children. The six-year-old's name is Beibei. Wake her at 7:45, then help her wash up, get dressed and eat breakfast. Get her to school by 8:20 and pick her up at one in the afternoon. Haohao, the baby, is three. Get him up at nine, take him to daycare at 9:30, and pick him up noon. The mornings are a bit hectic, but as long as you stay on schedule, there's plenty of time. Start dinner at three o'clock and take the children to the park for an hour at 4:30. They need a bath when they get home. Oh, I forgot to introduce you. This is my mother. She lives in San Francisco. My father comes to pick her up every weekend and brings her back Monday morning. She had a stroke, but the worst is over, although sometimes her mind's a bit confused. She has quite a temper, so don't let what she says bother you. You have to get her to do her daily exercise and take her medicine on time, go for short

78

walks, and take a nap. Most important of all is don't let her eat anything! She's on a strict, one-meal-a-day diet..."

As far as things like doing the washing and cleaning the house, there was no need to spell them all out. What it boiled down to was, she devoted every minute of every day to the family, and no point would be served by trying to remember every detail. On the first day, as she was washing the old lady's underwear and making her bed, she felt demeaned and saddened by her new status as a 'maid.' Then when she was trying to get the reluctant little boy out of bed, he mischievously said to her, "I won't let you dress me if you cry," and she realized that her face was covered with tears. It didn't bother her so much that she had to wash the baby's dirty behind, or fasten a belt around the old lady's waist, or get down on her hands and knees to play horsy with the children; what annoyed her was how low she had fallen. If she changed her status and helped her friends or colleagues with the housework, although the work might tire her out, at least she'd feel good about herself, especially since she'd be doing a good deed. And even if she was being taken advantage of, it couldn't possibly make her feel as inferior as she felt row. It's only a job, she thought encouragingly, an hour's pay for an hour's work, so why let it get under your skin like this? But that didn't work. When the old lady, the family's invalid, called out "Auntie, come help me wash my hair" or "Auntie, go see if Haohao finished his bowel movement," even though she smiled and did as she was told, a strong sense of shame made her loathe the old lady, who never took her eyes off her, and loathe her own impoverished, backward country. She decided to call one of her friends, just to talk, in order to channel off some of these feelings of loathing; but she'd no sooner dialed the first two numbers than the big-assed, large-faced old lady, warned her loudly, "Auntie, you have to get my daughter's permission to make a long-distance phone call..."

"Don't worry, I'll pay for my own phone calls!"

"Yes, I'm sure, but do you really think you'll remember them all?"

"Yes!" she spat out through clenched teeth, without a second look at the sick old grandma. After feeding the children at noon she poured a glass of juice and put a couple of pieces of bread into the toaster for her own lunch, just as the old grandma shuffled into the kitchen and stared at the soft drink and turkey sandwich Shan Naiwo had prepared. "I never drink a drop of juice," she said, both as a lesson for Shan Naiwo and a reminder to herself.

"Afraid of getting diabetes?" she said icily.

"The ham's for the children."

She kept her mouth shut to avoid saying something she might regret. She paused, then picked up a jar of bean sauce.

The old grandma grabbed it out of her hand and read the label. "We're saving this for braised tofu."

"There ought to be something I can eat, maybe some dog shit!"

"You people from China are always so blunt. I was just reminding you to eat right."

Shan Naiwo was determined not to say anything more; by then she'd also lost her appetite. Feelings of shame over having fallen so low as to become a maid in a strange land struck her again with full force and crumbled her resolve.

"Auntie, I'm calling you!" the six-year-old Beibei shouted.

Keeping her anger in check, she walked into the children's playroom, feeling like a balloon floating above a needle poised to pop her if she wasn't careful.

"Auntie, I want to play movies."

She nodded, hoping that playing with the children might make her feel better. She knew, of course, that in front of their parents the children acted like spoiled little tyrants to show their disdain toward a servant. But they needed and obeyed her when their parents weren't around.

"Auntie, I'll be the mommy, you be the daddy, and Haohao will be the baby, okay?"

She nodded again.

"How come you never say anything, Auntie?"

Um. She nodded, knowing that if she said anything the floodgates would open.

"Let's play being married. It's bedtime." Beibei climbed up onto her leg and pretended to get undressed and turn out the light, then wrapped her arms around Shan Naiwo's neck and said "I love you!" in the sexiest voice she could manage. She planted a kiss on Shan Naiwo's neck, wrapped her legs around her thigh, tensed her buttocks, and began to squirm. It was so disgusting it made her skin crawl. About to give the little girl a scolding, she wondered if she should check to see if she had a rash or roundworms or something on her behind. But then she recalled all the trouble the girl had given her that morning while she was trying to dress her, and just watched her strange movements with cold detachment.

"What about me, Auntie? What am I supposed to be doing?" the anxious Haohao asked her as he mounted her other leg.

"Don't call her Auntie? She's Daddy, and you're the baby," Beibei said, pushing her brother away before returning to her copulation routine.

"Auntie... Daddy, what should I be doing?" Haohao howled tearfully.

81

"Kiss her bottom."

Haohao obediently went up and kissed Beibei's bottom, which made Shan Naiwo more disgusted with herself than with Beibei. Pulling Haohao away, she told him to get his blackboard from the living room, and she'd show him how to draw a fish.

"Not a fish, a gun."

"Okay, I'll show you how to draw one."

"Auntie! Grandma's eating something!" Haohao ran back into the playroom shouting.

Shan Naiwo wasn't interested.

"Auntie, Grandma's eating a big piece." Haohao showed her how big it was with his pudgy hands.

"If you don't do something, I'll tell Mama when she comes home, and she won't let you eat at our house any more," Beibei mumbled as she continued kissing her.

All sorts of feelings welled up inside Shan Naiwo. She pushed Beibei off her leg and asked, "Would you like to be a nanny when you grow up?"

Beibei thought for a moment. "How could I? I don't know how to do all the things a nanny's supposed to do. Mama says you came here to be our nanny because you had to."

Shan Naiwo got up and ran to the bathroom, locking the door behind her. She looked at the dark, clouded face in the minor. No tears, no sadness, but in the depths of the eyes a spark of loathing.

The children's mother returned, bringing with her a group of bejeweled women like so many trinkets. Shan Naiwo stayed in the bathroom.

"Auntie. Where's Auntie? Bring us some lemonade, will you?" Mrs. Li said amiably, like a lovely serpent boring into her heart. She came out of the bathroom, prepared a tray of drinks, took a deep breath, and walked into the living room.

"Here, let me introduce you. This is our new auntie, a famous dancer from the mainland. When I was there last year I saw her picture on lots of calendars."

"Oh, the mainland!"

"If you were in Hong Kong, where I'm from, a famous person like you would be rich by now! Why are you working as a nanny?"

"It's not like you ladies think, "Mrs. Li said, signaling the trinkets with her eyes to stop the direction the conversation was taking. "She just arrived," she said, to put things in proper perspective. "She can't speak English and doesn't have a social security card, so this is the only job she can find. Besides, artists need to see all aspects of life."

Shan Naiwo reacted to Mrs. Li's attempts to rescue her more with loathing than with gratitude. Maybe they knew each other too well. With no visible reaction, she tuned and walked stiffly out of the room.

Mrs. Li stared in shock at her retreating back, but quickly regained her composure and asked sweetly, "Is dinner ready?"

Shan Naiwo nodded, barely.

"Make a couple extra dishes, would you? These friends of mine will be staying for dinner. And include Mrs. Wang's favorite, tempura."

Shan Naiwo didn't make any extra dishes, including Mrs. Wang's beloved tempura. Instead, she laid out the napkins, set the table, and brought out what she'd already made, then slipped out of the house, suddenly feeling good about herself once more. She sat down on a grassy knoll and looked up at the enormous sun in the western sky that was gradually being swallowed up in a sea of blood. As the sun disappeared from view, she was mystified by her own mood. Unsure if she felt like crying or laughing, she felt like sitting there forever. That common family wasn't going to order her around anymore. She'd call her girlfriend in New York and ask her to help. Deep down she knew it was hard enough for her girlfriend to take care of herself, let alone help a friend, and maybe she wanted to call just to reassure herself that to someone at least she was a respectable human being.

"Hello!" A black vagrant called to her, his white teeth showing between smiling lips, his light palm showing as he waved and began walking toward her.

Shocked and confused, she felt her heart race wildly; coughing dryly, she summoned up all her courage to glare at him and get slowly to her feet then began walking toward a row of houses. The black man followed at a distance. Not daring to turn to look or stop, she walked on as though she hadn't a care in the world. But, oh, how she wished that one of those front doors would open and an Asian — any Asian, even one who didn't speak Chinese — would emerge to restore her sense of security. But none did. At a bend in the road she spotted an old lady in colorful slacks watering a flower garden near her front door. She walked up and greeted her politely. Following a curt reply the lady lowered her head and continued what she was doing without so much as looking up. So Shan Naiwo plucked up her courage and walked into the flower garden, where she asked in broken English if she could use the phone, promising to pay for the call. The old lady looked up and said, "There are public

84

phones in town. It only takes an hour by bus." Shan Naiwo suddenly realized that it was an old man, not an old lady. He turned, walked inside, and closed the door behind him. She turned and walked away, frustrated. The black man, who was still standing a little ways off, smiled and walked toward her. In the midst of her panic, she thought of a young nanny she met every day when she picked up one of the children; she lived nearby. Another case of a financial guarantee that hadn't panned out: unable to afford her tuition, she was forced to get a job to pay for the coming school year. Although they'd only spoken once, there was a tacit understanding between them as fellow victims of hard times. She knocked at the door. As soon as the other woman saw who it was, she quickly slipped out the door and closed it behind her so her mistress wouldn't notice. She led Shan Naiwo away from the front of the house. "What do you want?"

"I'd like to use your phone for a long distance call. I'll pay whatever it costs."

The young nanny lowered her head in embarrassment and stared at the tips of her shoes. "Why not use the phone at your place?"

"I want to ask a friend to help me find another job, and I can't do that at my place."

"Not so loud. They're friends, and they wouldn't hesitate to tell. They have a rule that I'm not to bring strangers into the house."

"I sure don't want to make trouble for you."

"I'm sorry." God, if China weren't so poor we wouldn't be in this fix. She was still staring at the tips of her shoes.

Shan Naiwo appreciated the young nanny's logic, but spoke her mind anyway: "What does China's poverty have to do with a lack of backbone or spunk? Lots of Taiwanese leave good lives behind to become second-class American citizens!" She turned and walked off, the look of sympathy, apology, and timidity in the young nanny's eyes

85

etched on her mind. As soon as she was out on the street again she spotted the black vagrant, who was still staring at her. That's enough hiding and being afraid. She laughed loudly and swaggered toward him, shocking him so much he stopped in his tracks and stared dully at her. She waved, just as he had waved at her, and shouted out "Hello! Hello!" Maybe he thought she was crazy, like him, only worse. Still, he wasn't taking any chances; he tuned and walked away. She went back to the grassy knoll and sat down to gaze at the fading light of sunset, feeling as pained and empty as if someone had walked off with her heart. She was suddenly reminded of a Soviet film she'd seen in Peking a few years back entitled *Moscow Doesn't Believe In Tears*. But she cried anyway, before returning to the Li home, where she washed the dishes as she swallowed her tears.

Chapter 10

Some reporters turned up at school, looking for a student named Two. No one in any department bad heard of him. One of the reporters, a woman who refused to leave empty-handed, stationed herself at the library entrance, where she asked every Chinese-looking student who walked by if they knew who Two was. Someone said he might be Japanese or Korean, since it wasn't a Chinese name. One or two, suspecting a problem in the reporter's pronunciation, thought it might be Hu or Wu. The reporter insisted that he was Chinese, that he was a student here, and that he called himself Two. She took out a cloth-covered book and told the Chinese students gathered around her, This is a wonderful book, one of this year's bestsellers.

"What's it about?"

"Another Cultural Revolution book?"

The Chinese students' curiosity was piqued.

The reporter patted the cover and announced, '*Chinese and Americans Compared.*'

"Compared how?"

"Biologically, psychologically, culturally, behaviorally, even what they eat and how they feel about making love."

"So, we have a master in our midst. Don't look at us!"

"What's his major? Philosophy? Literature?"

The reporter opened the book and read the author's bio: Two, male, thirty-six, student from China. Current major field of study: America.

87

"What? What's that? He's majoring in *America*?"

Ha ha, they laughed loudly; all but one or two of them.

On a sudden impulse, the reporter asked the Chinese students to help her find Chen Chen, the president of the Chinese Students Association. He didn't know how he could help, but agreed to ask around at that night's showing of the movie *Evening Bells*. The reporter was grateful. They arrived at the screening room twenty minutes before the movie was scheduled to begin and asked the people in the audience. They were soon buzzing. Some thought it might be a pseudonym for Fang Yan from the Philosophy Department, while others guessed it could be Guo Shun from Theater Arts, who didn't want to use his real name. Even Jimmy Lu from Economics was suggested. Knowing how eager everyone was to see the movie, Chen Chen asked straight out, "Two, will you please identify yourself, so you can talk to this reporter and not get everybody upset." All of a sudden he froze. "Two!" he repeated.

"Two? That's English Er, isn't it?" Zhu Li and Chen Chen arrived at the same conclusion almost simultaneously.

"Impossible! That's stretching it too far!"

"It couldn't be him!"

"Don't be so sure. A weird guy like that's full of surprises."

As they looked around the room they spotted Two in a corner seat. His hair was long, as usual, his eyes looked slack, and the tiny body, encased in stone-washed jeans, was curled up in the seat. He looked like a prematurely aged child, his bewitching 'phoenix' eyes blinking rapidly.

Although the reporters didn't understand what was being said, they knew what was going on, and quickly surrounded Two.

88

"Everybody's anxious to watch the movie, so say something," Zhu Li said, giving Two an affectionate nudge to show that she and Two had a special relationship.

Two stood up and bowed like a movie star taking a curtain call.

The place erupted, as the other students swarmed around him.

"Mr. Two, I'm from the *New York Times*. Would you tell me why you call yourself Two?"

"Two is Er in Chinese. Is this some kind of joke?"

"What do you mean Er in Chinese?" the reporter asked.

"Er ganzi [stubborn ox], Er lengzi [idiot], Er shazi [fool], Erbaiwu [half-baked], Erban diaozi [half-wit], Er liuzi [bum], Lao Er [prick]," came a chorus of slangy shouts amid raucous laughter.

"Oh! Those aren't very good meanings, are they? What's your interpretation of Er, Mr. Two?"

"Er is different than yi [one]," Two answered stolidly.

"May I ask what you're going to do with your royalties, Mr. Two?"

"Bring my wife over."

"From Beijing?"

"No, she was sent down as a nanny in the States. She missed out on being sent down to the countryside in China when she was young."

89

The crowd around him erupted again. So, he's got a wife! And she's here in the States!

"Mr. Two, I'm from the *Washington Post*. What do you think is the biggest difference between Chinese and Americans."

"One's too shrewd, the other's too frivolous."

"The most important difference?"

"One's short on modem civilization, the other's short on cultural history."

The female reporter opened Two's book and began to read: "According to you, physical instincts tend toward frivolity, merriment, forthrightness, and comfort, while greatness requires profoundness, suffering, even war and upheaval. Life is a process of painful struggle between these..."

"No more reading. Ask questions!" "Who shouted that?" The reporter, undaunted, continued reading: "If a healthy child is the beneficiary of a mighty and weighty history and culture, he is enriched, becomes a deeper, more powerful person; but if the beneficiary is a weak, sickly child, he will mature too quickly and become confused and unbalanced."

"Stop that reading and ask questions." Someone else blasted the reporter.

"Let me finish this paragraph. You wrote: If a modern, scientific, blossoming civilization appears and is attached to an immature, turbulent group, they cannot see beyond wealth, resplendence, and frivolity. But if it originates in an ancient, somber body it can lead to epic glory. Instead of greatness, what China needs now is long-neglected mediocrity, wealth, and liveliness to meet the demands of its people's nature. China has fallen from its apex of splendor to its present state. After all these thousands of years my question is, will China ever regain its one-time splendor?"

Two looked up at the ceiling in silence.

A wave of agitation spread over the crowd — blondes, brunettes, and those with black hair.

Two gazed out the window into the distance, a benign expression on his face. He swayed gently, then nodded and sat down. His frail body, encased in stone-washed jeans, radiated the somberness of vast forests and icy glaciers, impenetrable, inscrutable.

The crowd settled down as the movie began.

Chapter 11

Someone, possibly the same woman reporter, found Shan Naiwo beside the bed of a paralyzed old man. She had opened the fly of his pajamas and taken out his shriveled penis. After watching him urinate, her face expressionless, she tucked the flaccid organ back in and buttoned up his fly. Then she washed her hands and his. "Are you looking for me?" she asked indifferently.

"Do you plan to return to your husband and get a fresh start?"

Shan Naiwo reached over to the old man's mouth with a sheet of powder-blue toilet paper and cleaned out some dark green phlegm he'd coughed up. Instead of tossing it into the wastebasket, she held it in the palm of her hand, looked at it for a moment, and asked the reporter, "Can he swallow this gob of phlegm again?"

The reporter stood there bewildered.

No Way out of China

Chapter 1

A height appropriate for five floors; they built six. Enough space for seven rooms; damned if they didn't squeeze in eight. Funds had been allocated to construct this little building to solve the housing problem for bachelor teachers, at the Eastern Academy of Dramatic Arts. But to create jobs for the sons and daughters of a dozen or more senior members of the academy and distribute bonuses to the teaching and administrative staff, they were forced to convert the first five floors into a guest house, leaving only the top floor — a freezer in the winter and an oven in the summer — for teachers old enough to qualify for individual housing, but who had been denied it owing to a number of housing committee regulations.

People meeting in the dark corridor of the top floor had to squeeze past one another. On Teachers' Day the workers union had sold off old desks at two yuan, one per person, and none of the lowly paid teachers could pass up such a bargain; now the desks cluttered an already narrow corridor. They were piled high with dog-eared books, old newspapers and magazines, boxes of waste paper, beer cans, and soft-drink bottles. Teachers with children also piled up wardrobes, crates, and seldom worn clothing in order to create more living space. The corridor became more and more like a gauntlet course. But even that wasn't enough to upset the residents, since they put their stuff outside their own doors, without taking up an inch of their neighbors' space. In fact, most people used up three or four fewer centimeters of their allocated space to show how broad-minded and unaffected they were. But this made it necessary to stack their stuff so high on either side of their doors that it was in constant danger of crashing down.

Six families lived in the eight rooms on the floor, with a communal bathroom and a twelve-square-meter washroom with three faucets, one for every two families. If a person walked in while someone else was washing up or brushing his teeth at his basin, he would wait, never considering using one of the others. The washroom served double duty as a communal kitchen. Along the wall stood seven kerosene stoves and two gas bottles. Several beat-up bookcases, convened into kitchen cupboards, stood at right angles, dividing the twelve square meters up into seven or eight cubicles of roughly equal size. But somehow gridlock was always avoided in the tiny room. The only family on the floor that followed a regular mealtime schedule was the loving young couple in 608; the others pretty much ate when they felt like it. But even the orderliness of the washroom took a back seat to the communal bathroom. Since there was only the one, it had to serve both sexes. Anyone heading to the bathroom, only to find the door closed, immediately retreated to his own room or to a corner in the hail to wait until he heard the toilet flush. Then if he met the person emerging from the bathroom, male or female, he'd nod politely to cover his embarrassment over having heard the sounds of excretion. As a result, no one ever barged in on anyone else at a delicate moment.

How, you ask, could a run-down place like that be considered an international corridor? Well, don't belittle the place just because of a few empty bottles and used newspapers, for it was a regular stop for foreigners of all types, including students; moreover, a steady stream of letters of invitation for overseas visits and study or immigration and settlement poured into the place. Its mood was like that of an enormous spring silkworm, whose threads could circle and strangle the world. One had only to listen to the Babel-like outpouring of English, French, Japanese, German, and other languages from tape recorders from the rooms to realize that the soul of this corridor had long since flown far from the confines of socialism.

Room 601 belonged to Huang Shizhi, a fifty-year-old instructor of long standing. Since his wife and child lived elsewhere, he had been assigned a twelve-square-meter room on the top floor. On holidays and special occasions, when his wife and child were visiting, he was confronted by foreign journalists and visiting China scholars who asked why he lived in such cramped quarters. He invariably responded by rubbing his pallid face with his hands, sighing, and saying, "Time, circumstances, the luck of the draw." The foreigners, finding it all very inscrutable, wouldn't know how to respond. Then his tiny wife — a flat-chested, bony woman who was somewhere between a normal person and a dwarf — would cross her legs, which didn't quite reach the floor, raise her head, with its broad cheeks and secretive appearance, and say, "Him? He's had a rotten deal! He finished his graduate studies in 1965 under Professor Tian Benxiang, the famous artist. While he was still a student he directed a stage production of the famous Japanese novelist Tanizaki's essay "*Hell Screen*," which caused a sensation in dramatic circles in China and Japan. *People's Daily* and *Mainichi News* even ran his photograph. Ah, but that was before we met." Overcome by emotions, she would shake her head sadly, her broad-cheeked head looking totally out of place on her tiny frame. Each time she proudly related this glorious page in their history to friends and foreign guests, Huang Shizi would be moved for the umpteenth time over the success of *Hell Screen*. His face would glow, his smallish eyes, which generally went unnoticed, would suddenly flash.

"Ah, I lost fifteen pounds over that play! I broke all the rules in format, turning it into a theater-in-the-round with audience participation. The lighting was perfect, blending with the plot, the moods of the dramatis personae, and the stage scenery to create a dark, distant atmosphere. As for the symbolic props, they were used with great success. Then there was the intent of the script. Under no circumstances would I permit the person playing the role of the painter Yoshihide to interpret him as an eccentric or a cruel painter, and certainly not as a head-in-the-clouds artist. In the scene with the burning carriage, which I accentuated by flooding the stage with a blinding red light, when Yoshihide saw his daughter's long hair go up in flames, like bursts of fireworks, his astonishment turned to grief, followed by convulsions as his soul flew out of his body. Then as he watched the transparent red flames engulf her body, his eyes opened wide and a tragic, cruel smile spread across his face. With raised arms, he looked like a man suspended from the heavens, embracing the essence of art and refusing to give it up. I told the actor that he was not just seeing his own daughter, but a human life at the majestic instant of being extinguished … throughout the dress rehearsal I stood behind the side curtain and didn't realize until after curtain calls

96

that I was drenched with sweat or that my face was streaked with hot tears. The actors flippantly said that I was the real Yoshihide. Ha ha."

Who could be unmoved by such a monologue? Leaving aside for the moment the question of whether Huang Shizhi was a dyed-in-the-wool artiste, it was clear that he'd been moved to the depths of his soul by the play. So anyone listening to him would not only sigh in awe, but would angrily curse a society that provided someone like him with such paltry rewards. At such times his expression would undergo a metamorphosis as he said, "Don't say that. A good dog doesn't mind that its master is poor, a good son doesn't mind that his mother is ugly. I've never said a word against the party, even in the worst of times. During the Cultural Revolution I was criticized for my name, forced to acknowledge that my surname Huang, in this case meaning obscene, represented my nature. But no matter how they beat me, I insisted that I was revolutionary red. My father was a revolutionary capitalist. Since the rebels didn't know what to do with me they started kicking me, breaking two of my ribs in the process, then in the hospital ordered me to write a self-criticism. I refused to budge from my contention that I was revolutionary red."

"See how stubborn he is," his wife interrupted reproachfully yet proudly.

"Nonsense. If I weren't stubborn I'd have traded you in long ago!" That was how he invariably responded to her, like a fly pecking at blood. The need for fame burned in the artist's breast like a hellfire, and if Huang Shizhi hadn't been a reasonable man, his tiny wife would long since have been pushed aside by one of the modem young students or a movie star who saw herself as the world's lover. Don't be misled by his ugliness, for he could talk with authoritative eloquence on stage plays, and had such uncommon qualities that no pretty face could begin to compare with his liveliness and brilliance. Take his beret, for instance. Since his son thought it was too gaudy, he had tossed it into a corner and stopped wearing it. But in the eyes of incoming students, for whom everything can be an, the beret gave Huang the aura of an artiste. Particularly the resplendent redness, which made him uniquely bohemian.

97

His tiny wife lowered her large face, with its high cheekbones, and sank into the bounteous sea of affection.

In 1980, Huang Shizhi, a ragged, unkempt man living alone in a township in far-off Ningxia, was transferred back to the drama academy, just when the winds of Sino-Japanese friendship were covering the land and blotting out the sun. The party committee decided that commencement services for the 80th graduating class of directing would include the performance of an avant-garde Japanese play to show they were up on the times. All the instructors knew it would be easier to find gold nuggets on a mountain than to be given the chance to direct a major play; except for the graduation play, the experimental troupe received funding for a major play no more than once every two or three years. So who wouldn't jump at the chance to actually direct a play? The only other way to win students over was through theory, which demonstrated the teachers' lack of self-confidence. Wolves were plenty, prey was scarce, and the teachers frequently bared their fangs in ferocious competition over an insignificant dramatic sketch or two.

Once in a while a major play was produced, based upon seniority; the chances that someone like Huang Shizhi would get the nod was unthinkable, except, maybe, in his dreams. But that's what happened this time. Associate Professor Ran Liao, who was in charge of the 80th graduating class, had been waiting impatiently for four years for just such an opportunity, and now it had come. But as luck would have it, an invitation from the University of Hawaii Drama Department to direct a play arrived, thanks to the efforts of his cousin, and now he had to choose between going abroad and directing the academy play. You don't have to be a genius to figure out which one he opted for.

A battle raged between the chairman of the department and his deputy, ending in a stalemate. The new academy president, Professor Hua Long, a compromiser with his finger on the pulse of public opinion, gave the nod to Huang Shizhi, as if it were the most natural choice in the world. Huang, who had recently arrived by

98

himself, had garnered the sympathy of his colleagues for the decade of suffering he had experienced, and his anointment as the director of the play not only made them feel better, but struck them as the best choice for the job. More importantly, it brought a fitting end to the struggle between the department chairman and his deputy. The elated Huang Shizhi couldn't sleep for nights.

The production was so successful it caused a sensation among Chinese and Japanese theatrical circles. Rumors were rife that Huang's peers at Waseda University in Japan had invited him for some guest lectures; his wife was included in the invitation. The female lead, Wu Yun, in the blush of her youth, had already developed a fond admiration for Huang's artistic qualities, at a time when nearly all the girls at the Eastern Academy of Dramatic Arts had crushes on their famous, and much older, male teachers, something that hadn't happened before. Day and night she hung around him talking about the theater and about feelings. On the night of the dress rehearsal she brought two cans of beer over to his apartment.

"This late, you?"

"How do you think the dress rehearsal went, Mr. Huang?"

"Not bad, not bad at all. Not bad, really," Huang replied perfunctorily as he buttoned up his shirt.

"Do you think I captured Natsuko's feelings?" She cut right to the main point without regard for Huang's reaction.

"Very well" He was relieved that they were talking about the play.

"Did I accurately portray the level of feeling when, after thirty years, she looked back on her youthful romance?"

"You were right on the mark! Just right. Just think, two people take a rushed vow, then struggle through the next thirty years, not meeting again until their hair is white. When they realize that the young lovers are now nothing but myths…" Huang Shizhi talked on and on, growing more excited by the minute, and forgetting his precautions against having a girl in his apartment this late at night. "Imagine the hurt, the sense of loss they must have felt. The exquisite portrayal of desolation and self-mockery in your performance couldn't have been better, especially when you laid your head on Mishima's shoulder and gazed weakly off into the distance teary-eyed. That, in my opinion, was your crowning glory."

"That's right. I was thinking of you at the time and why anyone would try to live a normal life with normal desires with a tiny little thing like your wife." Wu Yun gazed at him, the look in her eyes guarded.

"I won't listen to talk about my wife, the woman I love!"

"She's *not* the woman you love!"

"You're getting too excited. Go back to your room and get some rest." Seeing that Wu Yun's true feelings had surfaced, Huang's enthusiasm over talk about the play suddenly evaporated. By now he was an old hand at dealing with the emotionalism of these girls. Placing his hands on her shoulders like a father or older brother, he politely guided her out the door as though she were a little girl, flying to preserve her self-respect.

"You said you'd drink a beer with me as a reward for having captured Natsuko's feelings in the scene following theft separation," Wu Yun said, stubbornly remaining in the doorway.

"So I did. But it's late, and I don't have any beer."

"I brought some." she reached into her pocket and took out the two cans of beer.

"Okay, we'll drink them right now." He took one from her, opened it, clinked it against hers, and said earnestly, "Here's to your fine performance! And to our cooperation! Bottoms up!" He tilted back his head and chug-a-lugged the beer, all the while blocking the doorway with his large frame. Then he smiled wryly and shut the door. The next day he submitted a request to the party committee to have his wife assigned to the day-care center. Even though she was perfect for the job, he knew it would be the year of the monkey or the month of the horse before his request was approved.

Rumors are, after all, only rumors. Huang Shizhi did not depart on a lecture tour, to Waseda or anywhere else.

Several years later the Eastern Academy of Dramatic Arts was invited to send a delegation of four to Japan for a symposium on "Japanese Drama on the World Stage." Huang Shizhi was the first name that came to mind, for he had successfully directed two Japanese plays on Chinese stages. His participation was both fitting and understandable, and his nomination went unopposed. He was incredibly happy, for a time at least. In Japan he could see a number of plays and exchange views with specialists and directors from all over the world. He could also visit classmates and friends to gather material for a play of his own, which he'd have translated upon his return to China and, over summer vacation, produce with a small local troupe; he'd even have an old friend in the artistic section of Central TV tape the performance for national viewing. That would complete his trilogy: classical, modern, and contemporary Japanese plays. Once his position was secure, not only would his desire to direct be satisfied, but, even more importantly, he would gain advantages in terms of career assessment, salary, housing, and even the transfer of his wife to the day-care center.

When his thoughts reached this paint his heart nearly burst with joy. If others were present he would keep his lips tightly closed, so as to force back his great joy. As for the five hundred yuan they'd give him for expenses on his first visit abroad, he'd use that to bring his wife and child to Beijing for a few months.

Then his bubble burst! The participants list was pasted. The vice-president of the academy was to lead the delegation, which would include the chairman of the Directing Department, the elderly Shakespearean expert Xi Meng, and the interpreter Little Wu. Inexplicably, Huang Shizhi's name was missing. How absurd! Fit to be tied, he rushed over President Hua Long's home, and the moment he walked through the door he discovered that the look of distress on the president's face was more pronounced than his own. Hua Long grasped his hand enthusiastically before he could even sit down. After a moment's silence he said in a soft, intimate voice, "I was meaning to ask you over for a talk, but I didn't know what to say. I feel terrible about this. Even as president my hands are tied. If we'd had one more slot it would have gone to you for sure." He paused before continuing with obvious difficulty, "Ah, the vice-president's one of our senior statesmen, and after a lifetime of hardships and dedication, this is his first chance to go abroad. As for the chairman of the Directing Department, the play you directed should rightly have gone to him … " Hua Long's tightly closed lips and wrinkled brow spoke volumes to Huang about what had been left unsaid.

Mention of that play made Huang Shizhi feel as guilty as a man who had found someone's wallet and kept it for himself. He was frequently disturbed by thoughts like this, but he would quickly assume the angry attitude of a man wronged: What does someone who's directed a total of two plays in his career have to feel guilty about? And to whom? But after calming down, his thoughts drifted back to the department chairman; he felt sorry for the old fellow who had coached him in dramatic sketches and shown him how to improve his directing techniques.

As a young instructor reluctant to show off his talent, the man had unfortunately been labeled a rightist, and hadn't held up his head for decades. Returning rehabilitated only a few years earlier, he had been given the deserved opportunity to direct. But two officials charged with overseeing dramatic performances in the audience during the dress rehearsal were critical of the political implications and cancelled all public performances, awaiting further evaluation. Two years passed, then three, with no indication that the play would ever be performed. Huang Shizhi, on the other hand, had been rehabilitated less than a month before he was given an opportunity to direct, which even he had trouble understanding, even now.

Hua Long handed him a soft drink, but instead of drinking it he put it down on the desk, and while he was trying to figure out what to say, his eye was caught by a photograph of the premiere of *Hell Screen* under the glass cover of the desk. As his glance swept across the yellowing photograph, all he could think of were the reasons why he should be attend the symposium. He stood up, cleared his throat loudly, and said, "Hua *xiansheng.*" It had always been his contention that *xiansheng*, a term of respect for teachers, carried more weight than President or some other official title.

"Am I to assume that Xi *xiansheng* is going to Japan to undertake research on Shakespeare?"

"Sit down, just sit down. She's the reason I want to talk to you. Old Xi has spent a lifetime doing research on the plays of Shakespeare, but last year when the Shakespeare Research Center gave China a slot, Hao Hezi from the Youth Academy of Dramatic Arts was chosen. The vice-president and I went to the Ministry of Culture and the Dramatists Association, but we got nowhere. Hezi had recently directed a performance of *A Midsummer Night's Dream,* for which he'd received the Ministry of Culture Directing Prize. Besides…, besides, the vice-minister himself made the selection." Hua Long stopped there, restraining himself from going more deeply into the matter. He picked up his teacup and brought it up to his lips, but stopped short of drinking and gazed silently out the window. His reputation as a distinguished artist was well deserved, and his body language was all Huang Shizhi needed to understand the depth of his regret over what had happened and the distress he felt over his inability to rectify the situation, no matter how much he wanted to. His teacup became a prop in the scene, vividly representing the mood of the man holding it. What could Huang say now? Xi Meng *xiansheng* was not only his teacher, but Hua Long's as well, someone who enjoyed high prestige and commanded universal respect in theatrical circles. If, disgruntled, he fought over her inclusion on the list, he'd be seen as a petty man who had no understanding of the situation.

103

"You're still young compared to Xi *xiansheng*. Government policy is getting more liberal all the time, and your chance to go abroad will come. But the old *xiansheng* will be leaving us this year, so this is probably her last chance. Besides, she's a fan of Japanese drama..."

Sadness gripped Huang as the image of a young Xi Meng in the classroom flashed through his mind: English words covering the blackboard behind her, silver-framed glasses on her fair face, Ph.D. chain hanging handsomely from the earpiece beside her ear, swaying with her rhythmic movements and glinting in the light. Huang obtained his first sense of elegance and nobility through looking at Xi Meng, and it was through her that he came to appreciate the attraction of a woman of intelligence. Don't forget, one of his female fellow students whispered to him, Xi Meng's an old maid who was determined to return to China after her graduation from Cambridge to set up a drama school, while the man she loved went to Italy to study at the Far Eastern Drama Research Center ... who knows, maybe he'll be at the symposium in Japan ... lost in his fantasies, Huang Shizhi forgot his reason for coming.

"Old Huang..." The sound of Hua Long's voice stunned him. His thought processes went into suspended animation for a long while.

"Is there anything else I can help you with?"

"Oh, um, no." Huang Shizhi stood up to leave, and Hua Long warmly escorted him downstairs. After walking up the six flights of stairs to his room, as Huang inserted the key into the lock it occurred to him that the drama symposium was an academic conference, not an occasion for resolving personal relationships or seeking psychological balance. If those were the criteria for selecting the participants, it constituted an abrogation of responsibility toward scholarship and the host country. Without a moment's hesitation, he turned and headed back to Hua Long's, who placed his hand heavily on his shoulder before he could say anything, and started talking about something quite different.

"I knew you'd be back. Next May the Swedes are organizing a Strindberg Drama Festival and the academy will certainly be invited to participate. A major Stockholm theater wants someone from China to direct an avant-garde Chinese play. No one in the academy understands Swedish. Now you don't have any classes next semester, do you? Well, there's going to be an adult education course in Swedish in the Academy of Language Arts over the winter vacation..."

Everyone knows that education, health care, unemployment, and other forms of relief are guaranteed in tiny Sweden, with its laid-back lifestyle, and that students from Third World countries don't have to worry about food or shelter, and are eligible for interest-free loans as well. One young teacher sent for his wife and child before he'd been there six months. Huang reacted to the news by recalling everything he'd heard about Sweden and the Swedish people. He even had a vision of traveling to Sweden, which would resolve his family's residence problem.

Hua Long raised his eyes slightly as he tried to gauge what was going through Huang Shizhi's mind. He wanted to show his guest the door, but tried not to be too obvious in his speech or actions. So he stared at Huang and repeated his earlier question, with the same warmth in his voice, "Is there anything else I can help you with, old Huang?" Huang Shizhi knew it was time to bring the conversation to an end. But while he said "No" he was trying to think of a way to let Hua Long know how badly he felt about losing the chance to go to Japan for the symposium, so as to enhance his chances of going to Sweden later. How should he bring up the issue of Sweden? If he took the direct approach he'd seem too eager. But if he said nothing it would leave him feeling empty. Finally he walked to the door, stopping with his hand on the doorknob and one foot out the door to say casually, "Hua *xiansheng,* do you think I can learn Swedish at my age?"

105

A look of distress spread across Hua Lung's face, but just for a fleeting moment, before he smiled amiably and said, "You can learn at any age, as long as you go about it the right way."

Deep down Huang Shizhi was pleased, since Hua Long's affirmation of his ability to learn Swedish implied consent. So he pushed his boat along with the current with the response, "Don't worry, I'll work very hard."

Hua Long's brows twitched a time or two as he tried to distance himself from Huang Shizhi's plans: "There was a piece in the paper last year about a stay-at-home retired cadre in his seventies who decided to study a foreign language and made considerable progress in less than a year. Learning a foreign language will do you good. Well, I'll be in touch if something comes up." One inside, the other outside. One covering all the bases, the other feeling like a kite with a severed string. As Huang Shizhi walked out of the white building where Hua Long lived he was like a man adrift. He felt lightheaded, his legs were disappointingly rubbery. The streetlights had just come on throwing misty shadows on the ground, giving him the illusion that he was in the middle of the ocean, with no shore in sight. The only thing that was real, the one thing he could pin his hopes on, was the broad face in that tiny township in far-off Ningxia.

Chapter 2

"Lights, lights! Spotlight, side lamps! Flood the stage with purple to give it an air of mystery and melancholy."

"Director Mu Kun, are you flying for a new effect?" Big Liu asked as he covered the light with a filter and aimed it at Mu Kun, who was gesturing frantically.

It had a violent, uneasy, starving effect on everyone.

"Thirsty again, Director Mu Kun?" Big Liu asked in an overly serious, overly solicitous tone as he walked up.

Ignoring his customary sarcasm, she said, "The color's too light, Big Liu. Either use darker paper or a double thickness." She walked to the wing and looked up at the strips of gunnysack and threads of sodden plaited grass forming a net above the stage, then said to the art director with a sigh of disappointment, "You and I still aren't communicating! I'll explain one more time. The scenery's too realistic, too obvious. It has to be less substantial, more abstract. We're trying to suggest not mimic. We can't plant a fresh green tree on the stage, roots and all, just because it's in the script. But if we hang a piece of red fruit from a string, the audience will take it for a fruit-laden tree or blazing emotions…"

"A heart filled with longing, a sigh stretching across the Pacific Ocean," Big Liu recited poetically to illustrate Mu Kun's comments. But she didn't let his enigmatic outburst disturb her train of thought. Like a feathery boat, she glided past him and continued to instruct the art director: "Make the gunnysack strips as colorful as you can. Don't worry about distortion. Since it's artistic truth we're after, the scenery should evoke a state of mind, an atmosphere, and circumstances. Forget your hang-ups, try for a breakthrough. Use any color you can think of." But the old art director just kept working, neither looking at her nor answering her, like a zombie oblivious to what was going on around him. Finally she gave him an ultimatum:

107

"I've invited the cultural attaches from a few of the embassies, some Beijing reporters, and a couple of old friends from Central TV over for a forum, plus some interviews and stories, after tonight's dress rehearsal. I want you, sir, to carry out my vision, no matter what. We can resolve our differences in private, okay? Now take down those strips of gunnysack and dye them while there's time."

"Director Mu Kun, how do you expect us to go into the water on a cold day like this?" Wu Yun asked with a worried frown as she gazed at the shallow pool on the stage.

"That's exactly the stimulant we're looking for!" Big Liu said with a forced smile. "New and fresh! Isn't that right, Mu Kun?" His snow-white teeth gleamed.

"How are we going to recite our lines if our teeth are chattering?" Wu Yun asked with the tortured look of Christ on the Cross.

"Life's not supposed to be easy, little Wu. A famous actress once had her front teeth pulled just so she could act the part of an old lady nearing the end of her life." When she talked about art, Mu Kun seemed entranced by her own sincerity.

"Director Mu Kun, what sort of bonus do we get for going into the water during the coldest days of winter? I'll do anything for money. Don't forget, I want a bikini, too." Big Liu's face was still devoid of expression, but he worked without letup, carrying out Mu Kun's wishes faithfully. Once the stage was set, Mu Kun inspected it and sighed with equanimity. Then she went into the lounge to wait till curtain time. She took off her army overcoat, under which she was wearing a loose flannel overshirt with white stripes. At important moments in her life, she always wore this overshirt, which had been sent from across the Pacific; it gave her increased confidence in whatever she said and did. Maybe it served as proof of her prospects of traveling to the United States, and proved she hadn't been abandoned by her husband, who had washed her feet, rubbed her back, and willingly done whatever she asked of him at home.

Since selling off their belongings and borrowing what he could, exchanging it for U.S. dollars at the black-market rate to finance his studies abroad, his stock had soared, while hers had plummeted. It had been two years now, and she hadn't been abandoned by her husband, who washed dishes and cleaned toilets to get by; to some it seemed miraculous. There are always some people who place their hopes on others' misfortunes. At first everyone commented on her good fortune, but before long they were praising her husband as a man of character and high morals. What she found unbearable was how her friends and relatives, including her mother, asked when they met her:

"Gotten any letters?"

"When's he going to send for you?"

"Don't wait too long. Long nights are filled with dreams. You'd be better off if you had a child."

Anxieties, inquiring looks, sympathetic words of comfort, all so disturbing and humiliating. Especially the old woman in the mailroom, who for years had showered motherly love on her when she couldn't hand her a letter with an overseas address at least once a week. Mu Kun couldn't bear the anxious, frustrated look in the old lady's eyes. As time went on, the thought of not receiving a letter from her husband struck fear in her, not because she missed or was worried about him, but because of the frightful pressure of the people around her. Dealing with this pressure was time-consuming and exhausting.

One day a student who shared living quarters with her husband dropped by to see while he was back visiting his parents, and even though he tried to dodge her questions, she had a nagging feeling that her husband had begun living with a rich girl. After looking at some supposedly innocent photographs of them eating watermelon, swimming, and enjoying a vacation, her heart filled with despair. If he had fallen for a younger girl, or a prettier one, or one who was more talented, she would be jealous and frightened. If he couldn't stand the loneliness of being away from her and visited prostitutes to satisfy physical needs, she would understand and forgive. But how could a man who only yesterday had been hugging her tenderly so quickly give his heart to someone else? Maybe the commercialization of people's emotions was already complete. She smiled, broadly, loosely, struggling to appear as calm as possible, which confused this friend who had let the cat out of the bag.

Why shouldn't I be calm? Hadn't everyone warned her about worse prospects soon after her husband left, whether they meant to or not? She stopped writing to him after the visit, but told no one of the terrible thing that had happened to her, viewing it, and all her other problems, as the stuff of life, swallowing them like food at a meal, to keep herself strong. After thinking things through carefully she decided that the only way to keep going was to seek a new life, new love, a new man. It was her right.

Even though the wild horse of thought can run where it chooses, in actuality she was a married woman, a director, and a teacher. A decent reputation and the need to be a role model for her students had dictated a particular lifestyle for her. If someday she were to live outside the prescribed boundaries and assume a different code of ethics, both she and the people around her would probably find it difficult to accept. For a while she vacillated between the choices available to her, unable to decide how to put the past behind her and strike out anew. When two of her girlfriends invited her to go to church with them one Christmas, she accepted, unclear if she was just curious or if there were some other unknown reasons. She even experienced a mild rush of excitement over the prospect. Her girlfriends helped make her up: white eiderdown jacket, white tight-fitting slacks, short synthetic leather boots, all very tasteful and very youthful. She was astonished by what she saw in the mirror. How could anyone abandon such an attractive woman? Hard to explain. A self-assured woman exudes charm in the way she looks and in the way she walks. As soon as she was dressed she and her girlfriends walked out into the snow like a tiny flock of feathery birds, chirping as they flew to the church, where a host of devotees was kneeling in prayer as altar candles flickered. From the balcony the languid sounds of a women's choir rose and fell in hymn:

Pure as jade, clear as ice, a body like crystal,
Perfect beauty, radiant luster,
Her remarkable feminine glory surprises no one,
Her joyful heart is filled with love.

The solemn worship hall was filled with an aura of purity and beauty, which seemed to cover everything in the world — the sun, the moon, water, fire — and swallowed up all human emotions and desires; it filled Mu Kun's heart with the cold fragrance of peace. She felt refreshed and renewed, and completely at ease, as though a mysterious force was gently and unknowingly drawing her heart upward. She gazed at the penitent parishioners around her through clouded eyes, some kneeling, others seated before confessionals on both sides of the worship hall. Her being was contained in the atmosphere of holiness; she felt that everything between men and women — good and bad, joyful and tragic — somehow belonged to a spiritual world beyond human control, where it was rendered insignificant. Thoughts of how eager she'd been to compensate for what she'd lost made her uneasy; she was embarrassed by the restlessness in her heart.

She walked into a confessional and knelt down, resting her face against the closed wooden window, her eyes shut as she waited for the moment of mystery to arrive. How long she'd been there she didn't know when suddenly she heard the window slide open and felt a gust of dry, acrid air rush toward her from a tiny round opening. Drawing back and opening her eyes, she caught a faint glimpse of the coarse and all-too-real face of a man.

"Let's hear your confession, child," he instructed her.

"My husband is a student in the United States, and he's forsaken me and his beliefs, his emotions…"

111

"What do you have to confess?" he pressed her.

"If someone destroys my true feelings and beliefs, it's tragic, of course. But what really scares me is the thought of destroying myself..."

"What do you have to confess?"

"I have a troubled heart, and I've considered avenging myself by doing the same things."

"Be specific."

"I want to choose a new life, new love..."

"You have to be more specific."

"Oh. I've been considering taking a lover or getting remarried, or making some other choice in my life... how does the Lord look upon something like that?"

"Are you a member of the congregation?"

"Yes, yes I am. A member of the choir," Mu Kun lied.

"Have you been baptized?"

"No, no I haven't?"

"All right, then, come back after you've been baptized."

Bang! The window slammed shut, obliterating the little round opening like a wall and returning Mu Kun to the chaotic world of reality. She sat there stunned for a long while, her eyes open, until suddenly she discovered a slip-on shoe sticking out from under the black curtain of the confessional. The dirty sole of the swinging shoe gave her the feeling that it had just returned from the free market, or a butcher shop, or the toilet, or a line at a noodle stand. There was something ridiculous, something comical about kneeling in front of this foot; maybe she really was a little lost lamb. As she stood to leave she heard an old man in the confessional to her right pleading in a quavering voice, "Dear Lord, let my son and his wife have a change of heart and treat us two old folks better." Then a woman knelt and, in a pathetic voice, asked the Lord to give her a son. Mu Kun's glance swept across a row of kneeling people, a sea of black heads. The place looked like a huge toilet, or a luxurious restaurant, where people cleansed their systems of pain and misfortune and hoped to fill the vacuum with things denied them in their lives outside.

She stretched her legs to ease the numbness and was about to walk back to where her girlfriends were waiting, when a yellow cloth sack like a butterfly net appeared in front of her. She looked up and spotted several old women wearing yellow church armbands holding sacks on long poles in front of kneeling parishioners. Mu Kun smiled as she reached into her pocket and took out a few coins, which she tossed into the sack. The woman who was praying for a son looked up, cast a blank look at Mu Kun, then continued praying to the Lord for something else.

"Everyone says the big-nosed foreigners all go to church on Christmas, so where the hell are they?" one of her girlfriends asked as she walked up.

"Hmph, let's get out of here!" the other girl said. "Let's go to the International Dancehall. It's right down the street." She held Mu Kun's hand as they squeezed through the crowd of people listening to the Christmas evening mass.

"It's too expensive, and they say Chinese aren't allowed. There's supposed to be a Thai hostess at the door..."

"Where's your sense of adventure! Her bloodline's had plenty of infusions from us Chinese! Follow me. Act like you belong there, like you were going to the bathroom or something."

113

Her girlfriends laughed as they left the church, and even though there was still a heaviness in Mu Kun's heart, the moment she stepped into the sumptuous dancehall and saw the flashing lights and colorfully decorated Christmas tree, the comfortable, inviting sofas arrayed along the walls, and the tables filled with soft drinks, she felt invigorated. All around her, blonde hair and blue eyes were moving to the foot-tapping, breathtaking, heart-thumping rhythms of loud disco and rock-and-roll music.

The few Chinese in the place were mainly girls, all heavily made up and fancily decked out. They had abandoned the modest, innocent girl-next-door look for the gaudy appearance of their Hong Kong counterparts. Flashy colors, every imaginable fashion. Mu Kun took a look at herself and her girlfriends and had to admit that Chinese fashion had undergone a fundamental change, having become quite faddish. She walked over and sat in a sofa in a corner to watch the Chinese girls, who were more Western than the Westerners, a sight she found emotionally and visually pleasing, and which led to the sort of contentment one enjoys after venting one's hatred. A disco song ended and was followed by a sappy ballad. The Chinese girls were asked to dance by Western men of all sizes and shapes — tall, short, fat, skinny — all but a few, who looked around anxiously. A young Asian man asked one girl, whose bristly hair was penned like a pug-dog, to dance. She declined. Trying to act like one of the foreigners, he shrugged his shoulders and raised his hands palms-up, smiled, turned, and walked up to a dumpy, middle-aged Scandinavian woman.

"What are you doing, hiding in a corner?" Mu Kun's girlfriends emerged from the bathroom shaking their wet hands.

"Let's move someplace where we can be seen, so the foreigners will ask us to dance."

"I like to watch. You two go ahead."

"My dear Mu Kun, don't be silly. It's a crime against humanity for a pretty woman to waste her charms! Ha ha! Come on." They took her by the hand, but they'd no sooner reached a spot under a chandelier when a foreigner the size of a horse rushed up and, through gestures, invited them to dance. One of Mu Kun's girlfriends followed him onto the dance floor like a little lamb.

"I'm going to introduce you to someone, so don't shy away. Oh, here he comes. He's a German student from our academy. Hi, Joseph, this is a friend of mine, Mu Kun. She's a director of experimental drama at the Academy of Dramatic Arts, where she also teaches in the directing department. Why don't you two dance." She put Mu Kun's hand into Joseph's.

Mu Kun was startled to note that her girlfriend's English, at least where social terms and conventions were concerned, was so good. The frail Joseph stared at her with naked fascination, as though he couldn't take his blue eyes from her for a second. Embarrassed, she quickly composed herself, smiled, and nodded. "How do you do," she said.

"How do *you* do!"

Her mission accomplished, the girlfriend turned to leave, but Mu Kun grabbed her. "Who are you going to dance with?"

"Oh, Jack from the American Embassy is waiting for me." She freed her arm and walked toward a man with protruding bald spots. Although Mu Kun was uneasy, she followed Joseph onto the dance floor to the accompaniment of the soft strains of the ballad.

"What plays have you directed?" Joseph's Chinese was nearly perfect.

"Just a few sketches, like '*The Withered Man,*' '*The Red Wall,*' '*My Right Ear*'..."

"Oh, I've seen them all." Obviously pleased, he pulled her closer. Although her first reaction was to pull back, it seemed

115

excessive with the frail young man. So she smiled tolerantly and eased back slightly.

"I liked '*The Red Wall*.'" Grasping her hand tightly, he pulled her close again, his warm breath caressing her face. Mu Kun felt her heart shiver and it took everything she had to keep calm; she forced herself to think of something else to keep her turbulent feelings in check. But the more she tried to drive out the feelings, the more tightly they gripped her. But as a woman of class, she quickly came up with a thought whose implications were sufficient to deflate these feelings: You're acting like a baby! Once again she eased back, imperceptibly, until there was some space between them, following the action with a slightly motherly question: "What are you studying here?"

"Puppet theater... Chinese."

"How old are you?" The way she asked him drove away the last vestige of burgeoning romantic feelings.

"Twenty-five."

"Oh, you're still a child."

Joseph's long eyebrows fluttered a time or two to show his displeasure. Fixing his gaze on her face, he said, "I wish you wouldn't treat me like a child."

Mu Kun gave him a casual, passing glance. His eyes never left her face. The music seemed to congeal at their feet. Mu Kun raised her head until their eyes met. Since the day she turned into an appealing young woman, her gaze seemed to radiate enough heat to melt a glacier. But this time it was met by one of blue innocence that held its own blazing fire, eyes that seemed to radiate flames without a trace of impurity and looked like pools of crystal-clear blue water etched into his face above the high bridge of his nose. Mu Kun saw in them the alluring reflection of her smiling face... What time was it? How many songs had they danced to? Neither of them knew. The

116

limits of their existence seemed to be dancing, gazing, feeling. Mu Kun's heart had been aroused by the purity of his eyes, which were a repository of truth, a vast stretch of life-giving green.

The lights darkened abruptly, first turning blue, then yellow. The dancehall was like a first kiss — soft yet electrifying. Mu Kun was immersed in the magical flickering shadows around her. She felt a cool nose brush against her face, her eyes, her neck... finally stopping just above her burning lips... she turned her face away as gently as floating gossamer. To keep from shocking him out of his youthful dream, she calmly watched the swaying dancers around her.

A gyrating, closely pressed couple glided past her. The girl, in leotards, was resting her head on the chest of a brown-skinned, small-headed man, although her undulating gaze was fixed on Joseph's blonde hair. Another couple glided by, pressed together — faces, chests, groins — bodies swaying like a performing cobra. Was that her girlfriend? Mu Kun steered Joseph closer to get a better look. Her movements may have been too abrupt, for his eyes snapped open, like an angel descending from the kingdom of heaven, and he stared at her without moving. Another couple bumped into Mu Kun. Her? Mu Kun stared blankly at her other girlfriend, who was pressed against the chest of the balding Jack. Her rounded hips swayed vigorously, looking very sexy beneath Jack's thick, greedy fingers, like a wicked, seductive, hypnotic flower about to bloom in its perversity. Mu Kun felt like jerking her girlfriend's hips away from his beer belly, felt like snapping all ten of those fingers, with their eleven bejeweled rings, felt, more strongly than anything else, like yanking out every last red hair from the back of his hands!

"I'll be waiting for you Wednesday night in my dormitory room," Mu Kun heard her girlfriend say from behind her. "I want to buy some greenbacks."

"Seven point eight to the dollar."

"What? That's the black market price."

"No, I mean seven point five. What am I supposed to do with all that RMB?"

"Buy some needlepoint. Or some Formula 101 hair-growing tonic. You can sell it for ten bucks a bottle in Taiwan."

"That's strange. When did you get into business?"

"There are a billion and a quarter people in China, seven or eight hundred million of them in some kind of business. What's so strange? Now, don't forget to bring me an application form."

"Okay, my dear. Now, how about letting me spend the night."

"Not tonight. We'll see after our greenback transaction Wednesday night."

"You certainly are mercenary."

"And you're not?"

She wasn't aware that Mu Kun was eavesdropping, nor was she stimulated by being pressed against the man's body. In a clear voice she pressed her advantage in a manner that would make an accountant proud. Mu Kun suspected that the sensuous swaying of her hips was a biological action born of habit. She shivered with the realization that the air of this warm, cozy dancehall was alive with personal goals and deceptions. As she glanced around she saw that all the Chinese girls were plastered to the bellies, concave or convex, of Western men — including her, of course. Her initial sense of shame soon turned to sadness. If only China weren't so poor and so backward; if only it weren't harder to go abroad than to climb to heaven and embrace the moon; if only there were no sumptuous dancehalls that catered to the pleasures of these ox-headed, horse-faced Western men; if only poverty didn't get in the way of ideals; if only the Chinese people could extinguish their seven emotions and six desires, like religious devotees; if only the closed-door policy were still in effect, so there'd be no knowledge of Foreign Exchange Certificates, U.S. dollars, imported automobiles, and Coca-Cola; then maybe these girls from decent families wouldn't be prostituting themselves and selling their emotions and chastity so cheaply! Those men with their red or blonde hair who walked so easily in and out of the Beijing Hotel and the Friendship Store, heads held high, chests thrown out, might, for all she knew, be a bunch of untalented halfwits; but the minute they stepped foot in China, they became the personal embodiment of nobility and wealth, humbling the Chinese in the process. Mu Kun bit down on her lip as the ache in her nose was nearly stifling.

"Don't you love me?" Joseph asked anxiously as he squeezed her hand.

"Do you love me?" she responded icily.

"More than you know, from the moment I laid eyes on you."

"Swear to God?"

"Um... love you... it's..."

"Say it, swear to God! If you're lying, China's god will rip out your tongue!" Unable to control her feelings of disgust, her eyes bulged from the anger welling up inside her. Frightened by the sudden change, Joseph didn't know what to do. He merely shrugged his shoulders as his blue eyes flashed.

"Say it!" The sharp edge to her voice scared him.

"Not to love on Christmas... a sin."

"Clever little Joseph," she said as she patted him hard on the shoulder. "Do you think you're worthy of enjoying a sumptuous dancehall like this?" she asked coldly, withdrawing her hand from his and heading for the door, abandoning him and the dancehall.

119

"Hey, don't you want me to teach you German?" he called as he ran after her.

Mu Kun shook her head faintly as she wrapped her scarf tightly around her neck and rushed out into the snowy night, where snowflakes swirled in the vast white panorama. She forged ahead, leaving footsteps in the snow, some deep, some shallow. *Am I turning into a little old lady? Is it possible I'm no longer able to keep up with new trends? Did I over-react? Was I being too serious, too earnest? Maybe my husband across the ocean was at that very moment embracing his blue-eyed, blonde girlfriend... maybe in today's world what I witnessed in there is as common as the air we breathe and the sunlight shining down on us. Was it worth getting so wrought-up, so uneasy over?* Her mood was like the swirling snowflakes, chaotic and uncertain. As she turned the corner and passed by the tall gray wall of the church she heard the slow, muted sounds of an organ and the crisp, pure strains of women's voices:

Light emanates from the Holy Mother's body,
Her clothing white as autumn dew.
Eyes raised to heaven, a long sigh,
A look of melancholy on Her face.
Man more sinful than ever,
Bringing pain to the heart of my son.
All that must change
Before the Lord makes an angry appearance on Earth.
... Send your heartfelt prayers Heavenward,
... Ere mankind sinks into degradation.

Lord! Ha ha. The smile was still frozen on Mu Kun's face when she woke up the next morning. It seemed to make her a new woman who no longer agonized over emotional highs and lows, who no longer felt a need to seek anything or to make choices. She wanted to devote all her energies and feelings to projects that strengthened her. She was a woman whose ideas and actions moved in concert; strictly speaking, she had only feelings, powers of comprehension, and impulses, no real ideas. Given to impatience, in days past she had felt that making herself attractive was the first priority, followed by her work as a director. But at some point an invisible power forced her to reverse the priorities. "A director's worth is determined by what happens on the stage!" she reminded herself, gritting her teeth in determination. So she busied herself searching for scripts and opportunities to direct, wearing out shoe leather and talking herself hoarse as she sought out everyone who could help her produce a play, humbling herself by pleading, if necessary.

Finally, owing to a combination of personality and appearance, she received support in the form of 5,000 yuan outright and an interest-free loan of 10,000 more. By pleading with gramps and begging grannie, by trying every back door and connection possible, she managed to hire actors from the academy experimental dramatic troupe and rent a rehearsal hall without going over budget. But there was no way she could stretch the 15,000 to cover scenery, costumes, theater costs, and actors' salaries, forcing her into the position of having to pay it off with the proceeds from ticket sales. And since making a profit was important, she'd have to cater to audience tastes, which, these days, were as practical as nice, spicy bean curd or plenty of meat and fish; they expected to be entertained and pleased for their two-yuan admission price. To hell with sacred, lofty stuff! Who needs coloraturas and Beethoven? What do they have to do with us? Each age has its own art. If that's art, why isn't this art, too? Art evolves along with people. Mu Kun had the right idea, but she was reluctant to give up her seat in the traditional Palace of Art, the chair reserved for true artists.

She was determined to produce a play that would satisfy current tastes, please the leadership ranks, and at the same time avoid criticism by her fellow artists that she had sold out. No easy task for little Mu Kun the director. The two months of struggle that followed so exhausted her that even though she wasn't spitting up blood, she felt as though a couple of layers of skin had been scraped from her body. But just when she'd pushed her body to the limit, her efforts were crowned with success. As the curtain rose she felt like a woman

121

at the birth-giving moment when the pain and agony vanish; the only thing missing was the gratification of seeing her newborn infant.

Her body slack to the point of collapse, her mind completely blank, she didn't have the heart to watch the performance, choosing to return to the lounge, where no one could find her. But a stagehand came and dragged her backstage, where she paused and looked out blankly on a sea of pale yellow faces beneath a floating layer of pale yellow expression; disgust welled up in her heart. An orange spotlight shone down from above stage right to lower stage left. Moonlight? The fading rays of sunlight? A young man and a young woman in bathing suits jumped into the pool on the stage, where they frolicked intimately, splashing the stage around them. The startled audience began to stir.

From somewhere in the audience there was a shrill whistle, drawing Mu Kun's attention to the sea of shaking heads in front of the stage, which suddenly went dark, covered by a purple light. A group of dancers in flesh-colored costumes came onstage performing a martial-arts dance, their faces expressionless, their movements mechanical. The audience grew still, and she didn't have to look to know that the play had reached the point where the male and female dancers face each other and, with slow, exaggerated movements, act like they are kissing. The audience erupted in applause. Mu Kun closed her eyes and smiled, mumbling derisively, "You people, I can make you do whatever I want. This is what you came to see, isn't it?" She turned and walked up to the log keeper, who said hoarsely, "They're into it now, and they'll probably go crazy at the disco number." Before his words had died out, Mu Kun was inattentively heading back to the lounge. As she rounded a corner she was brought up short by the sounds of a commotion nearby. The sight that greeted her was of several reporters holding microphones up to Huang Shizhi.

Huang Shizhi? Why are they interviewing him? Mu Kun was puzzled.

122

"Content should dictate form, and is therefore more important than form!" Huang Shizhi sounded agitated; his red beret floated above the people's heads, bobbing contentedly.

"I have nothing against a bunch of ragged gunnysacks or rotten grass hanging above the stage as a gaudy external display. The tragedy is that they express outmoded intent and consciousness. All this nonsense that love is giving, that uncultured peasant girls are pure and decent, that good conquers evil... how sorcery and trigrammatic divination show people the way..., sure, you can dress up your actors in miniskirts and bikinis, but even if they shout themselves hoarse, they're still singing the same worn-out tunes..."

"Foreigners are sick and tired of that crap!" Huang Shizhi's critique was cut short by the shouts of some youngsters wearing badges of the Eastern Academy of Dramatic Arts.

In truth, foreigners like nothing more than watching plays written on themes of ancient Chinese customs, like *The Sorcery of Young Master Dog* and *The Divinations of the Fairy Princess.*

"Okay, okay! It's like visiting natural preserves to see a bunch of endangered species! We're Chinese, and we ought to be concerned with life in modern China and modern techniques, not continue to dredge up vulgar customs that have outlived their usefulness just to cater to foreigners!"

"What difference does it make if the customs are vulgar or if they've outlived their usefulness? That's a sociological issue, and giving them artistic expression implies no obligation to please external ideals. Art is art. You don't have to tell the audience that this is shit, this is piss. It's like a flower. When you give it to a friend it symbolizes friendship, when you give it to your sweetheart it means love, when you place it on a dining table it enhances the appetite, when you lay it on a grave it's an expression of mourning..."

"Nonsense! A flower's an inanimate object that grows and is nurtured in the ground, but art is nurtured by people, with their goals and their desires, and traces of people are never absent in it..."

"When art derives from man it becomes an independent entity..."

"The world, human nature, theory, and philosophy are all rounded. It's the age-old question of which came first, the chicken or the egg."

"Teacher *Huang*, let's hear your views on the dancers," a reporter said as she thrust her microphone up under Huang Shizhi's chin.

"I believe that the artistic form of a play should take on its own unique characteristics." Huang's comment seemed to lie in his throat just waiting to be released, whether a reporter asked the appropriate question or not. "You and I, for instance, are talking face to face now, but if we were in a bedroom and I was facing the window as I said the same thing, the two settings would represent a different personal relationship, a different state of mind, and different implications. Ideology, mood, and consciousness are all embodied in dance in today's plays, at the expense of the unique nature of spoken drama, until all we see are operas, ballets, and variety shows."

Just then a round of shouts and thunderous applause from the audience abruptly swallowed up Huang's comments. The reporters turned and rushed back up to the stage, leaving Huang Shizhi standing alone. Mu Kun knew that the play was reaching its climax, but what concerned her were the doubts that had crept into her mind over the meaning of art. Maybe the nature of art really did change. The disco music had begun. Forcing back her repugnance, she walked out of the darkness up to Huang Shizhi, and as their eyes met she discovered that, with the exception of an excitement over drama, there was nothing to see in his eyes; she immediately forgave him for his attack on her play.

"I'm surprised to see you here, Teacher *Huang!*"

"I know how hard it is to get a play staged, and how all kinds of practical factors have made it impossible for you to realize your ideals as a director..., but it seems to me, it seems to me, oh, somebody's looking for you. I'd better go." His unsolicited apologia made her feel unbearably guilty and threw her heart into turmoil.

"Teacher *Huang,* we've arranged a forum for after tonight's performance. It won't last long, and I'd be honored if you'd attend and repeat what you just said, word for word, for the video camera."

"No, no, I was just spouting off because I was excited, just spouting off."

"Don't worry, I wouldn't let a forum on art turn into a farce. I'd like you to attend, please."

"Well, all right."

Huang Shizhi was moved by Mu Kun's open-mindedness and magnanimity, which made him feel petty and small-minded, like a fleck of dust on a garbage heap. If anything, she was more moved by her own attitude than he was. She was always trying to formulate a speech the likes of which the world had never seen, one that incorporated a radiant artistic sensibility, was free and easy, spontaneous yet capable of moving someone to tears. Self-aggrandizement was a flaw in her personality. Even at her worst she viewed this bigger-than-life person she had imagined herself to be as standing head and shoulders above her billion and a quarter countrymen, an extraordinary human being, one of God's truly magnificent creations.

The audience filed out of the theater, talking and laughing among themselves, like a puddle of stagnant water covered with foul bubbles flowing into the sewer. Mu Kun was carried along by this filthy water all the way to the exit, where a TV reporter was interviewing a red-faced young man and woman on the air.

"Tell me, please, what was your impression of the play?"

"The disco scene was great! It was like they did it for a living."

"Kissing like that in full view of everybody broke down all our traditional taboos."

"Why did you come to see it?"

"The evening paper said it'd be a great show. I'm an old friend of traditional spoken drama, and this is the first time I've ever seen anybody actually jump into a pool on the stage."

"How about you folks?"

"Heh-heh, let's see, how should I say it. Conditions are too crowded at home, and the park's too cold, so the only way we have a relationship is by going together to movies and plays."

That caused a stir among the growing crowd.

"What about this older gentleman here?"

"It takes a lot for somebody to go swimming on a cold day like today! It's always been hard for actors to make a living."

"Great! That was some play!" a brash young man announced forcefully as he squeezed through the crowd up to the camera.

"There goes Big Huang, trying to get on TV!" shouted one of the young men crowding around the TV camera.

"It was vulgar, unspeakably vulgar! Now you see the kind of people this play was meant for!" This aloof, critical comment came from one of two girls wearing white school badges as they passed in front of the camera, keeping their faces turned away.

126

"Wonderful news, Director Mu Kun! All three performances are sold out!" little Liu, the stagehand, reported as he forced his way up through the crowd. "I'm going out to buy a couple more cases of Coke for the forum."

"Is she the director?"

"Mu Kun's a woman?"

Gazes like daggers were suddenly directed at Mu Kun, who felt as though they were passing right through her, leaving her body filled with sieve-like holes, out of which a red liquid seeped. She couldn't have felt more embarrassed or more unhappy, like an ugly girl paraded in front of a crowd to hear their critical comments. With lowered head she made her way out the exit, where she was met by a blast of frigid air like an icy shower. She let out a long sigh, as though relieved to be in a quiet place away from the raucous world behind her.

"No, I want one more popsicle!"

"Don't fuss, be a good boy. You'll get sick if you eat too many."

"Okay, but only if you give me a kiss."

"Come over here, my little darling."

Mu Kun felt a lump in her throat in the darkness, goosebumps covered her arms. Naturally she didn't think women should try to appeal to men by acting like little girls, but she was deeply moved by this little episode by the loving young couple. Not wanting to spoil their dreamlike tenderness, she softened her footsteps. Like all dreamers, sooner or later they'd have to wake up, especially in times like this, when it was no longer possible to float along on a dreamy river of love. As she looked up at the cold,

127

cheerless stars surrounding the Milky Way, the emptiness in her heart frightened her. Tears slid down her cold cheeks.

Chapter 3

Big Liu, a strapping young six-footer, was turned to putty by the gentle softness of snow. Strange though it seems, fine snowflakes nearly melted his steely heart when they touched his face. The snow-covered ground was the embodiment of a beloved wife and pampered daughter, whose red lips and soft white hands caressed his state of mind. Maybe that was because he hadn't yet ventured onto the ancient, casualty-strewn battlefield of married life, even though he was over thirty. He gazed at the snowflakes swirling around him, unsnapped the collar of his parka and unzipped it to facilitate the tender sentiments between the snow and him. He wished it had taken longer to get to the back of Beihai, for now it was time to cast off the good feelings he'd been enjoying and dive into the icy water.

In virtually no time he had stripped down to a skimpy pair of swimming briefs and a blue bathing cap. He was ready. After rubbing snow on his body until it turned red, he stepped over the barrier and dove into the watery hole cut out of the ice. As he swam he rubbed himself all over, until the painful pricks of the icy water turned to a suffusing tenderness that really got his blood pumping. He took a deep breath and dove to the bottom, producing a dizzying sound as water rushed past his ears. It was warmer down there than on the surface, and more peaceful. Only at times like this he could wipe his mind clear of everything, like an infant lying in the palace of maternal love. He rose to the surface again and gazed out through the mist floating above the water at the snow-covered riverbank and the heavily dressed pedestrians walking back and forth. He felt vital, proud. He dove to the bottom a dozen times or so, until he grew tired, then floated on the surface, as delicate snowflakes landed on his warm body.

Suddenly he felt lonely. Why hadn't she come? Ever since winter set in, the girl in the red bathing cap had shown up at the same time every day, whether the wind was blowing or snow was falling.

They'd never spoken, never really looked at each other. A nod, a smile, that was the sum total of their greetings. He always spent more time in the water than the girl, who merely dove in, splashed around for a moment, and climbed out. At first he'd felt pity and a general aversion over this routine of hers. A girl's a girl. She should be like a flower blossom, or a rosy cloud, or a fragile vase, to be placed on a pedestal and admired by others, instead of subjecting herself to such a cruel physical and mental regimen. But after a while he got used to it and his aversion evaporated. Every time her steamy body, like a crystalline, nearly transparent, object, emerged from the water, he had a vision of feminine beauty impossible to see in the office or out on the street or in the arms of a man.

On the day of the year's first snowstorm he rose at the crack of dawn, even though he had a terrible cold. She wouldn't come out in weather like this, he assumed with a smugness that made him feel superior and excited him at the same time. When he arrived at Beihai he looked around and felt as though he was master of all he surveyed. But then a blazing spot of red appeared in the white panorama, floating above the broken pieces of ice. Fiery hot, blinding. Amazement, jealousy. Maybe an emotional bond was forged at that moment, for from then on the blazing spot of red seemed often to alight on his heart.

He swam longer than usual. What's happened? Why hasn't she come? Sick? No, not her. She'd be here even if she were a little under the weather. The more he pondered why she'd missed her morning swim, the more chaotic his mood grew; after climbing despondently up onto the ice, he dried himself off slowly, then wrapped his towel around his waist to change out of the wet trunks into his street clothes, and threw his parka over his shoulders.

"Hi there." She emerged from a clump of bushes weighted down by snow and ice, like an angel descending. Crystalline snowflakes were stuck to her white down overcoat and glossy white scarf, to her bangs and eyelashes. Her smile was like a snow-covered winter lotus, waving gently in the morning breeze. For the first time

130

in his life he understood that a woman's smile could be as pure as the driven snow.

"You, why aren't you swimming today?" The growing turmoil in his heart kept him from saying more.

"I've come to say goodbye." Her gaze passed over his snow-covered shoulder into the vast panorama behind him, sadness in her eyes.

"You?" The news floored him. His refreshing swim and the closeness of the girl, so close he could smell her fragrance, how could it end just like that? He wouldn't let himself believe it. But the absurdity of that thought made him laugh inwardly. Maybe she's married, or maybe she has a boyfriend. I'm nothing to her. Since she probably is married, or has a boyfriend, a lovely morning like this and my feelings of contentment have nothing to do with her. But his heart was pounding. It took a while, but he calmed down and asked in a friendly, brotherly tone, "Why not take a dip?"

"Oh!" The single word conveyed a heavy sadness, a deep sentimentality like everyone experiences once in a while, not just someone who's saying goodbye. She took her knitted red bathing cap out of her coat pocket, fiddled with it for a moment, then said confidently, "Want to trade? Like a souvenir?" He quickly wrung the water from his cap and handed it to her. Trying to appear natural, but succeeding only in coming across as very stiff, he said, "I get the best deal, since mine's only nylon."

She smiled — a lovely, radiant smile.

"Where are you going?" he asked reluctantly.

"Paris."

"For school? What will you be studying?"

"Fashion design."

131

"Originally you studied…"

"Philosophy."

"Are you planning on becoming China's first doctor of fashion design?"

"What's important, of course, is to become the best fashion designer I can be."

"Ah, a master in the making!"

"Heh-heh. You're a teacher in the Department of Art Design at the Eastern Academy of Dramatic Arts, aren't you?"

"How did you know?"

"Oh, your red school insignia, the paint splotches, and your long hair."

"You have a philosopher's head. Making clothes, isn't that a little too, you know... but maybe it's fashionable these days."

"Heh-heh, someone told me once that by reading my book you can discover the insignificance of the world and the significance of the individual. Someone else said that through my philosophy you realize there's no philosophy in the world, that philosophy is nothing but silence. In response I told them not to try to figure out the laws of the universe. Philosophy is nothing more than a product of man's fears and pains, his struggles, self-consolation, and escapes. You have to work to be happy..., oh well, goodbye!"

"Goodbye!"

With a heavy sense of mystery and a feeling of reluctance he followed her with his eyes until she vanished into the snow and mist, finally coming to the realization that everything in his past was irretrievable. He smiled in spite of himself, wrung out his swimming briefs, and stuffed them into his pocket. Feeling restless when he returned to the dormitory, he picked up a newspaper and read it inattentively. When that proved fruitless, he crumpled it into a ball and tossed it to the floor, then ground it with his foot and spun around, cursing angrily, "How can this god-damned country of ours cause such suffering among its billion decent, upright citizens! Me, a language student? I should be lecturing at the University of Sydney!"

"Has the tuition for the Australian Language Institute gone up again?" Blackie asked Big Liu as he peeked out from under the eiderdown comforter with his little rat eyes.

Big Liu didn't say a word as he took a barbell out from under the bed and curled it a dozen times or so. Blackie emerged from under the comforter, picked up the newspaper and crawled back in. "The application fee has doubled in less than two months," he said emotionally after reading for a few minutes. "It's no longer good enough to pay half a year's tuition up front. Now they want you to send enough to cover room and board before they'll admit you. When you add in the cost of the plane ticket you re looking at a minimum of 4,000 U.S. Then if you can't get a visa, they refund the money to your university, not to you personally, for you to continue your studies...

Big Liu put down the barbell and wiped his sweaty face wordlessly. Blackie took a cigarette from the headboard, lit it, and stuck it in his mouth; then he made an ashtray out of an index card, which he put beside his pillow. He lay there in deep thought.

"Why does everybody rack his brains to find a way to get to Australia if it's so hard to do? Not long ago the president of an Australian university came to China on a fact-finding mission. They put him up at the Far Eastern guesthouse, and the next morning the place was surrounded by hundreds of young Chinese. Some came to offer their services, some to pick up application forms, and some even brought Maotai, chinaware, diplomas, and transcripts, hoping to sneak in the back door. It's so sad. The world's afraid of the 'yellow peril'!"

This sort of meaningless grumbling disgusted Big Liu, not because he disagreed with the complaints or had no feelings for his country or its people, but because he couldn't stand his friend's cherished rebelliousness. Blackie's one-act play, *China, You Lost The Key*, performed by students from the Normal University Drama Troupe, had been shut down by school authorities because of references to corruption within the party and how bureaucratism was running wild. Later on, news of what had happened somehow reached the ears of the wife of one of China's ambassadors, who invited Blackie and some of his students to her home, where they acted out some of the scenes, to their hostess' appreciative delight. She quickly organized a small party, to which she invited the cultural attaches from a number of embassies, a few Sinologists, and some reporters, who raved over Blackie's play.

Word spread like wildfire, and the incident quickly took on the earmarks of a major cultural affair. A Hong Kong publisher brought the play out in book form, including a tantalizing editor's blurb on the cover to attract buyers: "Following its unauthorized premier performance inside China, this play was placed on a list of proscribed works. Its author, working in an extremely repressive environment, has wrestled with fundamental issues of humanity and society, showing inevitable trends in the rise and decline of various social systems." This increased the book's worth so much that even people inside China tried everything possible to get their hands on a copy. The incident resulted in increased contacts between Blackie and a number of foreigners, whom he treated with extreme courtesy and attentiveness, without sacrificing his self-respect and aloofness from mundane affairs. With his fluency in English, he was able to draw them to him with ease. And never did he so much as mention letters of invitation or financial guarantees around them. It was they who brought the subjects up, to which he responded in a reserved tone, "Thank you, I'll think it over."

Blackie's lofty, unyielding demeanor, his gloomy concern for his country and her people, and his rebellious opposition to China's traditions, bureaucracy, and the current state of society frequently earned for him the admiration and sympathy of his foreign friends. A collection of his plays was translated into dozen or more languages and published by commercial presses in North America and Europe, gaining him an army of readers throughout the world, and a respectable income in several foreign currencies. In response, the academy's party committee assigned him a two-room apartment as an expression of its willingness to tolerate and protect a variety of different views, and even assigned him a bed in Big Liu's dormitory where he could rest during the day when he was at work. By and large this served as equitable compensation for his efforts and the generated income.

None of this, however, had any measurable effect on his gloominess and grumblings; if anything, they increased. It was almost as though they constituted the sole worth of his existence. He grew more and more outspoken over inequitable aspects of society and corrupt practices within the system, until he became a hero in the people's eyes. The authorities reacted to his insults and ostracisms with smiles that masked their bitter loathing. As an expression of approbation, he was made deputy leader of a delegation of popular agencies scheduled to go overseas on an official visit, allowing him the opportunity to express his opinions and discuss his works with his foreign counterparts, which, they hoped, would erode his mysterious appeal in the international arena.

But Blackie was a clever man with plenty of tricks up his sleeve. He refused all titles and special treatment, asking only to remain an ordinary teacher in the Writing Department; he entertained foreign guests in his three-man dormitory room — only when Big Liu and Baohua were out, of course. Sometimes Big Liu came into the room when Blackie had guests, but the normally courteous and attentive Blackie never once bothered to make introductions. In time Big Liu came to understand the subtle reasons for this. At first he refused to believe that Blackie was duplicitous, and that his suspicions were unfounded; but after this happened several times he

135

was forced to face the fact that he had been mistaken in not recognizing the real Blackie.

One Sunday an Australian scholar of the classical novel *Dream of the Red Chamber*, an old lady named Jennie, dropped by to sample Blackie's Sichuan cooking; they were drinking Coke and discussing the author of the novel, Cao Xueqin, obviously hitting it off beautifully. Big Liu had come to the dormitory from home, intentionally taking Blackie by surprise. No introductions. So Big Liu, feeling somewhat mischievous, stuck out his hand and introduced himself to Jennie: "I teach in the Art Design Department. They call me Big Liu."

With a weak smile, Blackie patted Big Liu on the shoulder and asked with uncommon cordiality, "Why are you doing this to me?"

"Because I really like this woman," he replied with exaggerated earnestness.

The old lady, misinterpreting his candor and openness as genuine, reacted with warm interest. But as she was looking in her purse for a name card to give Big Liu, Blackie stopped her. "Eat up," he said in an unaffected manner, "you don't need to give him your card. I'll give him your address later tonight."

But Big Liu, who was enjoying the game, stuck around the dormitory room while they were eating, busying himself by flipping through magazines or making his bed. Blackie was like a man who'd swallowed a fly and couldn't bring it back up, but he couldn't be too obvious in front of the old lady. All he could do was switch from Chinese to English and freeze Big Liu out of the conversation. With that maneuver Blackie effectively lost the respect of Big Liu, who realized he was just turning Big Liu and the others' dissenting attitudes to his own advantage. Not that he was unmoved by Blackie's actions, for there was no denying Blackie's courage in taking Hua Long to task for his middle-of-the-road attitude toward art at an open meeting at the academy, and in complaining publicly that the

Communist party was infected with an incurable disease, and in living with a girl out of wedlock to see if they were compatible. He'd also had the courage to refuse the two-room apartment offered to him. Big Liu knew full well that Blackie was doing all this to benefit himself, but it still required guts to go through with it. If there were more people like him, maybe hypocrisy wouldn't be so rampant in China.

As Big Liu glanced at Blackie curled up under the comforter his mind was filled with strange thoughts. He walked over to the corner of the room that was screened off by a sheet of plastic and some plywood. When he pulled back the screen he spotted Baohua sprawled face down on his bed, stark naked, examining his body with two large hand mirrors. Finding the scene incredibly funny, for some reason he still couldn't laugh. Apparently oblivious to Big Liu's presence, Baohua lifted up his right leg and put one of the mirrors down by his crotch, then raised the other above his head so he could get an unobstructed view of the slack skin hanging down. After studying himself for a few moments, he lowered the mirror and his leg at the same time, then scribbled something in a notebook. He sat up, spread his legs, and lowered his head as far as it would go, trying to see how close he could put his mouth to that thing that always stayed hidden … his eyes were bulging, producing the look of a bull that's spotted its favorite cow. Big Liu edged up closer and landed a resounding slap on his friend's icy rump. Baohua's head jerked up, his mouth hanging slack, as he stared at Big Liu dumbfounded.

"Why the hell don't you go over to the department and draw one of the models?"

Baohua smiled sheepishly.

"Because they're jealous of you?"

Baohua just smiled, like a simpleton, and climbed under the covers. "My muscles are degenerating," he said with closed eyes, "and more lively."

Big Liu smiled dryly and gave Baohua a shove.

"I need some help."

"What do you need?"

"I want to design some beggar's shirts with colored patches. They have to be unique, matching the colors just right so they'll really sell."

"I don't follow."

"I'll make a pattern and promote them at clothing stalls. They pay for the material and the cutting, using my design, for a 70-30 split. That way you won't have to strip naked in freezing weather to draw yourself."

Baohua was staring wide-eyed at Big Liu without, it seems, seeing him. "Why waste your talent and energy on something like that?" he said sadly, as though talking to himself.

"Fuck you! Literature, art, politics, economics, they're all as goddamned worldly as anything else! Like a bunch of whores, people are only too happy to sell their emotions and lives for these worldly things."

"What does that mean?"

"It means talking about high and low, noble and common is a bunch of nonsense. Are you going to help me or not? You'll get an honest ten-percent cut."

"You're missing the point. I can give you a hand, but I don't want a cut."

"I won't be obligated to anybody. I'll pay you for what you do, no more, no less. That way there won't be any bullshit later on."

Big Liu took out some patterns of his beggar's shirts and handed them to Baohua. "The only requirement is that they be anti-traditional, something no one's seen before. Each pattern can only be used for a few shirts, and all the color combinations have to be different."

Baohua reluctantly took the patterns and studied them for a moment before taking out a brush and knocking off a few dozen designs.

Big Liu stood behind him while he worked, constantly praising him: "Good!" "Great!" "Lots of red and green, make them as bright as you can, real eye-catching! That's right, anti-traditional, as anti-traditional as you can make them. For thousands of years the ideal in clothing has been neat and well coordinated. Well, we're going to be revolutionary as hell, with loose threads all over the place. I'll tell you, brother, you've got talent. Your designs are terrific. I'm going out to drum up some business."

Big Liu rushed out of the room and downstairs, several steps at a time, to the telephone booth on the ground-floor guesthouse. Blackie was already there, his parka thrown over his shoulders, his feet in his shoes with the backs turned down, as he spoke into the receiver in English. Big Liu was burning with impatience, but Blackie closed his eyes and kept talking, as though he'd never finish. When the female attendants heard Blackie speaking a foreign language they listened as though they were hanging on every word. A couple of them walked around the telephone booth as though looking for something, while the others mopped the floor or dusted tables, walking back and forth in front of Blackie.

"I have to use the phone for a minute," Big Liu blurted out impatiently, nudging Blackie.

"Excuse me," Blackie said into the phone, "I'll get back to you in a few minutes." He hung up and moved over to the windy hallway.

139

"It's cold out there. Wait inside. I'll only be a minute."

"I'll wait out here. Tell me when you're finished."

"It's freezing. You don't have to show how civilized you are." Big Liu smiled.

But Blackie closed his mouth tightly and stood in the freezing hallway without moving.

He dialed five numbers. Three times he got a busy signal, and no one answered the other two. He looked at Blackie, whose head was scrunched down in his parka, and decided to try one more time. Finally a woman answered, but he no sooner asked her to put someone on than she said "Not in!" and hung up. Slamming down the receiver, he stormed out of the cubicle, forgetting to tell Blackie he was finished.

By the time Big Liu reached OK Street on his bike he was soaking wet. He raised his face to let the cool snowflakes fall on his overheated face, where they melted and formed a fine mist. He was surprised to find the place so crowded in spite of the blizzard. Profiteers wearing faddish clothes from their own stalls were hawking their wares with a bunch of "Halos!" Big Liu peddled up to the stall run by Chief, his classmate. Some Turkish or Pakistani women were holding up tie-dyed Chinese style jackets.

Chief held up his tape measure and pointed to the number 62, then said in halting English "six two." Either because they didn't understand him or they thought the price was too high, they shook their heads, shrugged their shoulders, and jabbered something to each other as they walked toward one of the other stalls. Big Liu, who had already taken Chiefs side, grew anxious when he saw them leaving; he walked up and called them back in English. Then he searched his guts and scraped his tongue to muster up as many English words as possible to point out the Chinese qualities of the jackets, like a disinterested bystander, plus the perfect color coordination and the fine tailoring. With sighs of admiration, they picked out the patterns they liked in their sizes. This led to a chain reaction, as a group of "amateur overseas Chinese" girls rushed up and began rummaging through the jackets. In no time at all, the dozen or so jackets on display had vanished. Chief stood on his tiptoes, wrapped his arms around Big Liu's neck, and nibbled hungrily.

"How much did you make?"

"Three hundred RMB and two fifty in FEC."

"Not bad! More than I make in six months."

"Let's have dinner at Kentucky Fried Chicken, my treat."

"No nonsense, now. I came to talk to you about something."

"I've lived to do your bidding since I was little. Out with it."

"Do you remember the last time I was at your house I told you my plan about beggar's shirts?"

"You're not thinking about lowering yourself to join our profession, are you?"

"Why not?"

Seeing that Big Liu was serious about joining up with him to sell wares, Chiefs heart sunk. He lowered his head and fiddled with his tape measure as he said, "You always did better in school than me, and the only reason I took up this line of work was because I failed the high-school entrance exam. Take a look at these guys. Just because they're so well-fed they ooze grease, how many of them have the education you've got?"

Big Liu raised Chiefs head, staring into his eyes as he said with determination, "I'll tell you, I'm not nearly as well off as you are.

141

You're able to buy a decent home for your parents, while my mother's still living in the same earthquake shelter she was in when my father was alive... The thought hurt him too much to go on. So he changed his tone and continued after a pause, "Besides, well educated can mean lots of things, including this."

Chief looked at Big Liu for a long time, as though in the grip of enlightenment or a sudden inspiration. He'd never looked this closely or this long at Big Liu. In elementary school he'd often been reprimanded by his teachers and parents for copying Big Liu's homework. Then in middle school he sat next to Big Liu, and when he was stumped, Big Liu held his test paper so he could copy the answers. Then came the high-school selections, and Big Liu gave up two summers to help him prepare for the exams. During his third year, Big Liu was selected for the Art Design Department at the Central Academy of Dramatic Arts, while Chief still hadn't passed the high-school exam. So two children who had grown up together in the same compound ended up differently, and the neighbors began looking at Big Liu with renewed respect. Chief, on the other hand, began distancing himself from Big Liu, who rarely saw him on his weekend visits to his parents.

At first Big Liu went to Chiefs house to wait for him, but he soon discovered that Chiefs self-respect suffered when he did that, not to mention the disappointment his parents felt. So he stopped going to see him, and on those occasions when they met, their contact was limited to a brief nod of recognition.

Once the free markets opened up, Chief set up a small shop to develop color film, and in less than three years he'd made over a hundred thousand yuan. His home was equipped with every imaginable electric appliance, and the walls were covered with expensive calligraphy. Hearing that there was FEC to be earned at OK Street, he turned the film-developing business over to his younger brother and set up a clothing stall. He may not have done well in school, but he had an instinctive grasp of foreigners' tastes in Chinese clothing. At first he sold military greatcoats, then he turned to coarse, hand-knitted sweaters, from which he earned a tidy sum of

FEC. When other stalls selling military greatcoats and hand-knitted sweaters began turning up, he started selling tie-dyed Chinese skirts and checkered cotton blouses. The previous year alone, before going into the cotton-silk skirt business, in less than two months he had a net income of over 10,000 FEC.

Now that he was rich and generous, he helped Big Liu's mother financially without telling anybody. For her sixtieth birthday the month before, he and the neighbors each contributed five yuan, as always, and bought her a new comforter cover and some longlife pears. Once the drinking commenced, pretending to be drunk, he walked over to the 9-inch black-and-white second-hand TV Big Liu had bought for his mother and twisted the dial until it broke. Big Liu couldn't see through the apologetic look on his face. Then a few days later, when Big Liu was out, he brought over a big-screen Hitachi color TV. When Big Liu's mother refused the gift, no matter how much he cajoled her, he changed his tactics, accepting the paltry sum of 200 RMB, saying he'd bought it at the factory outlet price. Big Liu was both moved and saddened by the incident, and finally had a taste of the reasons Chief had avoided him in their youth. Now he came seeking Chiefs help in selling beggar's shirts. Chief didn't know whether to believe him or not, suspecting him of having had too much to drink, since it was out of character for him to consider going into business.

"Do you really want to do it?"

"Yeah, I need the money badly."

"How much?"

"Two thousand U.S."

"What for?"

"I want to study, but I don't have the tuition."

143

"Study where?"

"Australia."

"Have you passed the test?"

"No need to. I'll go to the English Language Institute. They take anyone who can pay the tuition and has enough to live on."

"Even me?" The words were no sooner out of Chiefs mouth than his face reddened. Just thinking about the shame of failing the high-school entrance exam, and how Big Liu had spent all that time tutoring him, was enough to make him lower his head until his chin touched his parka.

"Of course, even you. You can start with the ABCs. Six months' tuition and living expenses are two thousand U.S. All you need is an acceptance letter to get a passport and a visa. But you can't put it off, or else the costs will go up."

"Really?"

"Really."

"After six months, then what?"

"No need to think that far ahead. Getting out is what's important. But to answer your question, after the first six months you can find some work while you keep studying. And there are other options. If one of those Aussie girls takes a fancy to you, you can get married and apply for immigrant status. There's a road under everyone's feet, as long as you keep walking."

"I can really go abroad as a student?"

"Why don't you have any faith in yourself?"

"I'm twenty-seven years old."

"Everybody has a chance to study."

"Okay, I'll get the money today! Two thousand, right?"

"U.S."

"Naturally. It's in the Fourth Eastern branch of the International Bank."

To Big Liu, the fact that Chief could go to the bank and withdraw that large a sum so easily was like a mosquito bite he couldn't scratch. Last year he had taken the TOEFL exam twice, scoring below 500 both times, which disqualified him from scholarship competitions at the U.S. universities he had contacted. To go on his own, which meant a financial guarantor, was beyond his means. Several years earlier, a classmate had received a passport to attend an Australian language institute by scraping together a mere $400. By working and going to school at the same time, he now owned a house, a car, a master's degree, and a good job. The shock and allure to Big Liu was like gold-rush fever for the Yankees or the rush for truth by Chinese who struck out for Mao's Yan'an. By borrowing and cajoling he scraped together RMB 2,000, which only netted him a little over $300 on the black market.

Finally, somehow, he had the $400 he needed, but by then the tuition and living costs for six months at the language institute had risen to $800. And the new goal was still out of reach when the costs rose to $2,000. I'll be damned if I go! he thought angrily. The year Zhou Enlai and Deng Xiaoping went to France on a work-study program in their search for truth, Mao Zedong stayed behind in Hunan to make revolution; they reached their common goal by different means. But look what was going on around him: All he heard were stories about going abroad to study and the first thing his classmates and co-workers asked when they saw him was, "Where do things stand with your application?" Then they'd tell him about someone who had opened an art exhibit in Norway or someone who had just received his Ph.D. in Hawaii or someone who was waiting tables and cleaning bathrooms to get by or someone who was teaching deep-breathing exercises in Chinatown … It would take him at least ten years to qualify for the limited number of government-sponsored scholarships. What about going abroad to visit relatives or friends? He poured over a map — the five continents and the four oceans — no family, no friends. Reluctantly he decided to find his future in China.

"Big Liu." Chief saw that his head was bowed and that he had grown silent. "I'll go first. I'll learn English if it kills me," he said, feeling guilty. "Once I earn enough and get a handle on the fashion industry there, I can set my younger brother up here to make some money selling the newest fads in clothes. Sooner or later we'll get another $4,000 together. And don't worry, I'll bring you out before him."

Big Liu grasped Chiefs hand tightly. "I have an application at home. I'll fill it out for you. A classmate of mine is leaving next week. He can take your application and money out with him and contact the language institute in person. You can probably expect your acceptance letter next month, then you can apply for a passport." Without looking up, he mounted his bicycle and started off. But Chief grabbed the rack and said, "When you've got the beggar's shirts ready give them to my younger brother."

Big Liu stomped down on the pedal and rode off like the wind. He refused to think about any of this for fear that despair would drain his energy, energy he needed to accomplish his short-term goals. As he passed by the People's Theater canteen his stomach began to rumble, so he dug out some change and bought a couple of yogurts, which he ate while he watched the people lining up at the box office. Blackie was among them, his head scrunched down inside his parka. For some reason Big Liu suddenly felt hot and dry all over, as though a demonic fire was burning in his chest and nearly suffocating him.

"Hey, why don't you get free tickets from Director Mu Kun?" Big Liu challenged Blackie.

146

Blackie's head emerged from his parka, but scrunched back down after a nod.

"Standing in line for one of your foreign friends again?" With a yogurt in one hand, he grabbed Blackie with the other, making it impossible for him to ignore Big Liu's vulgar behavior.

"Why don't you just ask for tickets?"

"It's not right."

"Afraid you'll compromise your aloofness? Then why stand in the snow as a foreign lackey?" Jealousy filled him like a mouthful of vinegar as he released a bellyful of filth onto Blackie for buying theater tickets, something that had nothing to do with him! But seeing Blackie chew his lip nervously was satisfying, so he tossed away his yogurt, mounted his bike, and rode off.

Blackie cast a panicky glance at Big Liu's silhouette against the snowy backdrop as his hand froze in the narrow box-office window, as though he'd forgotten to pull it out.

"Is your hand broken?" A girl in line stared at him angrily. He quickly withdrew his hand with the tickets.

"What's the matter, don't you want your change?" the ticket seller growled.

Blackie quickly took his change and gave his spot at the window to the girl, then stood sadly to the side as though frozen in the snow. Why's everybody in such a rotten mood these days!

Chapter 4

The curtain was rising slowly on a test of strength.

The invitation from the Strindberg Drama Festival had arrived, and the Eastern Academy of Dramatic Arts planned to enter a play. The word on the grapevine was that the Chinese-born wife of a Swedish Consulate official had said that if the play did well, the director and principal actors would be invited to speak or participate in cultural exchanges throughout Scandinavia. Who could pass up such a tasty morsel? The party committee gave the assignment to the experimental drama troupe. Now which play? And who to direct it? These questions were on the lips of every person in the academy. Even though the experimental troupe directors were faculty members in the Directing Department, the troupe was autonomous. One of the four active directors, who enjoyed considerable prestige and respect, was home sick a good deal of the time, while another was visiting relatives in California. That left Huang Shizhi and Mu Kun to compete for the opportunity.

Mu Kun got busy on all fronts, while Huang Shizhi acted as though the job was already his. He searched the reference section and the library for photos and other materials on performances of *Miss Julie* in various countries. But his main concern was choosing an actress for the title role. His mind was working overtime as he pondered his choice, but none of the actresses in the experimental troupe seemed right for the part. Lacking the inherently noble character of Julie, they simply weren't up to the task. Not even the finest director can draw qualities out of someone to whom they don't come naturally. Wu Yun? No. She'd never had a role as complex as Julie, who had given herself to the servant Jean under the influences of family, tradition, the Christmas eve atmosphere, the pair of boots, the onset of her menstrual period ... it was totally beyond the capabilities of a frivolous young thing like Wu Yun. Without the ability to comprehend the character, she could never create the passion the role demanded. At best she was able to pander to an

148

audience enough to elicit a few worthless tears, and was best suited to exaggerated, dramatic moments.

Hu Nan? Absolutely not! Her assignment to the academy had been a mistake from the very beginning. Although sweet and moderately talented, she had no understanding of the acting profession. No matter what the role, it was always the same smile, the same expression. In her performance of the poetess Li Qingzhao she displayed the airs of a kitchen maid's daughter. When everything came together just right, at best she was capable of ephemeral stardom. In the wake of the Cultural Revolution, when literary and artistic circles lay in ruins, a single song, a solitary short story, an isolated film script could turn someone into a marquee star. Of course, before the Cultural Revolution, anyone who wrote fiction, poetry, or film scripts was referred to as "celebrated," a laurel whose weight could bow the head of the finest artist. Hu Nan had achieved "star" status because of her performances in two films. Now her portrait on calendars adorned stalls all over town, and in public toilets and bicycle parking lots students and loafers cinched up their belts and nibbled melon seeds or peanuts while they discussed her. And yet her qualities, her cultural level, her education, yes, even her damned fame, denied her the opportunity of becoming a full-fledged actress.

Chen Meng? Yes, Chen Meng, a girl from a good family who had gone through so much. She was a second-tiered actress who could assume many different roles with vivid precision … and yet … and yet the images she created lacked that special charm. She was incapable of creating a new character that was neither the actress herself nor an exact portrayal of the assigned role.

Huang Shizhi was just too demanding. He stripped the skin and flesh of every actor until their bones showed. This flaw had appeared on his very first day as a director. The roles from his scripts took on excessively mystical and artistic proportions in his mind, until actors found it impossible to approach the sacred qualities of the roles they were given, even if they stood on their tiptoes. His

149

restless search for actors for the roles of Julie and Ron cost him several sleepless nights.

Mu Kun was preparing Strindberg's *The Ghost Sonata,* a late play which, on the surface, seemed best suited to her tastes. With its mummies, corpses, and phantoms, plus the bizarre and unexpected plot twists, the heavily philosophical language, and the tone of mankind's spiritual crisis, the play afforded a director the chance to experiment with modernist techniques. She would strive for the maximum technical and emotional effects. Form, she often said, embodied content, and a play was like a sculpture: a particular form determined a particular content; another form led to a totally different content. She was determined to give the world a view of contemporary Chinese consciousness and artistic temperament. Her youth gave her a distinct advantage over Huang Shizhi. If her play made an impact in Sweden, her prospects for the future would outshine his: schools, lecture tours, jobs, marriage.

Once her goals were clear, the thrill of impending success imbued her with limitless nervous energy. For days on end she was like a windup car out of control, not stopping even when it lost a wheel. At this rate, both car and driver were imperiled.

She rose early, wolfed down a couple of slices of bread, photocopied the script, and headed straight for the reference section. At noontime, she passed up lunch to discuss her ideas with Hua Long while he was eating at home. To avoid antagonizing his wife, she summarized the two-hour play in twenty minutes and licked her lips as though she'd already had lunch. When she left Hua Long's home she went straight to a grocery store, bought a soft drink, with which she washed down a chocolate bar, and planned her afternoon. First she pedaled over to the Swedish Embassy, where, with difficulty, she was able to call on the Cultural Attaché's wife. When the formalities were over she cautiously broached the subject that was on her mind.

Armed with two videotapes of the Swedish National Theater performance of *The Ghost Sonata,* she left without so much as a polite how-do-you-do; but when she reached the academy and went to the projection room, it was quitting time. She pleaded, she cajoled, finally hinting at the gift of a carton of Marlboros, before the man in charge of the projection room handed over the key, demanding that she leave no later than 10:30 that night. With profuse expressions of gratitude, she promised to shut down the projector by 9:30 and return the key early the next morning.

Four hours of videotape watching later she walked out into the star-filled night, exhausted from the day's activities; yet the adrenaline flowed as she thought about how her play would soon become a reality, and what a wonderful piece of work she was. Instead of getting on her bike for the long trip home, she walked slowly, savoring the day's activities, all of which showed her talent and abilities in the best possible light, and recalling her witty, humorous comments.

"What are you doing outside on such a windy night?" Blackie was standing under a streetlight near the dormitory, his head scrunched up into his parka.

"Waiting for a Swedish friend."

A friend from Sweden! A new thought formed in Mu Kun's mind, and she stopped to chat with Blackie, as it became an imperative.

"Why don't you wait inside? It's freezing out here."

"The gateman has been watching the comings and goings of my foreign visitors like a hawk the past few days."

Mu Kun was well aware of the tension Blackie created for his foreign acquaintances, who preferred to meet him at the entrance to the park. She was about to make a sarcastic comment, but it was blocked by the new goal forming in her mind. Her instincts told her that somehow she'd enlist Blackie's help in this competition. It was time to share in his displeasure: "That's ridiculous! It's like they think the foreigners you meet with are all cultural spies!"

"You're aware of that, too?" He'd been dealing in deception so long that even he had begun to believe what he said.

"Even if it's true, everyone wants to see his own culture find its way to other countries. That's what cultural exchange is all about." She knew that Blackie loved homilies, so she racked her brain for comments that catered to that desire.

"Ah, China!"

"Um, I need your help with something?"

"Hmm?"

"I'd like you to translate *The Ghost Sonata.*" As the words emerged, the vague thought now took form. Maybe this was the first stage in its realization.

"Isn't there already a translation in *Selected Plays of Strindberg?*"

"It's flat. I'd like you to retranslate it from English."

"That's not such a good idea, is it?"

"Why not? There are plenty of translations of *Selected Plays of Strindberg,* and a director's free to choose the one she wants."

"Sure, I can ignore the original and do a good translation."

"With your excellent English and literary background, the translation will have everybody raving."

"Okay, I'll think it over. But it'll take a while. Won't that slow down production?"

"No, you've got a month."

Mu Kun already knew what she was going to do based on the original translation, and she only asked Blackie to retranslate the script because she wanted his name — more to the point, she wanted his participation. This was an important move in her quest for total victory. Blackie knew this, of course, for she wouldn't give him such an easy way to enhance his reputation without an ulterior motive. Still, it couldn't hurt, particularly since it was art, not politics, and he never refused an opportunity to display his talent. An unspoken agreement was reached.

Feeling slightly uneasy over her clever ruse, Mu Kun climbed the steps of the apartment block.

"I got us a butane gas bottle, Cousin." One of her younger male cousins was waiting anxiously for her at the door.

"Really?" Startled by the news, she didn't know what to say. Obtaining a butane gas bottle in Beijing is as hard as a healthy person climbing to the moon or a cripple finding the love of his life. Instead of opening the door to her apartment, she dragged the bottle up and embraced it hungrily with her eyes.

Oh no! It's a Mt. Fang bottle. It looks like a Beijing bottle, but the trademark's different. You can't get these filled! The crashing disappointment exceeded her initial excitement. Not only wouldn't they fill it, she was out 200 yuan for the bottle itself. The debts her husband had left her with still weren't paid off, so half her pay was docked each month. But when she saw her cousin's crestfallen look, she concealed her anguish and reassured him: "Getting a Mt. Fang bottle's quite a coup," she said matter-of-factly, then went to pour him a cup of tea; but both vacuum bottles were empty, it was too late to get boiled water, and she hadn't had cooking gas since last month.

Buying gas required getting up early and standing in line for the two catties allowed per purchase (and it could be weeks before you had a chance to make a purchase). She had neither the time nor

153

the patience to stand in one of those lines. She considered asking her neighbors across the way for some water, but when she saw the young lovebirds washing their clothes in the doorway, the man's forehead beaded with sweat, the woman looking like a penguin flapping its wings as she ran in and out, she changed her mind. Looking at her own bleak room, with its cold, empty vacuum bottles, she was struck by the realization that giving up life's daily pleasures and knocking herself out over a stage play, just so she could go abroad, seemed a little ridiculous. Neglecting such necessities as having enough food to eat and a bit of warmth in her matchbox-sized room, while getting so excited over a stage play, was either a tragedy or a joke. Of course, she knew she was being moody, like the tides, and that she'd feel better soon.

When she woke up in the mornings, with the new day's sun climbing in the sky, or when she saw the performance of a good play someone else had staged, no matter how exhausted she was she'd be filled with a desire to triumph and throw herself hell-bent into a new struggle. Her cousin sat off to the side silently fuming. Asking favors from friends, passing out good wine and cigarettes, even going so far as to carry a Mt. Fang gas bottle on the back of his bike, then wait outside her door for a couple of hours, all for nothing. He heaved a long, heavy sigh and said sympathetically, "Cousin, all this running around, is it worth it? Your husband doesn't know how to enjoy life, either. People nearing middle age should be enjoying life, not going to school!"

Mu Kun's eyes felt hot as she turned and said with a sneer, "He knows how to enjoy life. But everybody does it differently." She closed the door, putting the young lovebirds out of view. "Living near them can be very stimulating," she said lightly. "I ought to sue them for emotional distress." She thought that would make her smile, but it nearly brought tears to her eyes.

"Well well, aren't you the one! Mu Kun's got herself a Mt. Fang gas bottle," Big Liu said as he squeezed into the room while she was seeing her cousin out.

154

"Don't give me any lip! I can't have it filled!"

"Mu Kun, let's make a trade."

"What sort of trade?"

"I'll get your bottle filled for you, and you let me take part in *The Ghost Sonata.*"

"I was going to do that anyway."

"No, I mean let me be the art director, just me."

"You? Oh, what am I going to do about the gas bottle?"

"Does that mean I can do it? Get me a hammer, a knife, and a pair of pliers, oh, and a bowl of salted water. Come on, help me carry it out to the balcony. Come on!"

Sick people will do anything to get better. For some strange reason Mu Kun saw a glimmer of hope. On the balcony a northern wind stabbed their faces like daggers, but that didn't bother Big Liu, who stripped off his padded jacket, picked up the hammer, and banged it hard against the gas bottle.

"Have you lost your mind?"

"I have to bang it up first, then scrape off the paint with the knife. Then some salt water to let it rust."

"Why?"

"To make it look old. Then I paint on enough of the Beijing trademark to make it look real."

"Where the hell did you get a goofy idea like that?"

"From Professor Huang in the department. His family's been using a 1978 gas bottle all these years, but last year one of his students bought him a Mt. Fang bottle. He ran around begging gramps and pleading with granny, but no one would fill it for him. He was so mad he came up with this idea. He designed a tin Beijing plate, and it worked. We've already made a dozen or more fake trademarks for gas bottles at the academy."

"My God, even a famous, respected professor is driven to the point that he has to make phony trademarks!"

"Why so surprised? If he didn't solve his bottle-gas problem, who would? Okay, now once this bottle looks old enough, make sure you have it filled at night just before the end of the work day."

"Why?"

"They're in a hurry to get home, so they won't pay any attention to one beat-up old gas bottle. Check to see if the fellow on duty's a young guy. If it is, get pretty little Wu Yun to swap it for you."

"You've got everything figured out!"

"Okay, the paint's scraped off. Now splash the salt water on and let the wind and sun do their work for a couple of days. I'll borrow Professor Huang's tin plate and stamp your phony trademark for you. I guarantee you'll have gas next month. Now listen to my ideas on art direction for *The Ghost Sonata*."

"So you had this planned all along. What if I hadn't gone along with it?"

"Naturally I had other cards up my sleeve, other ideas, other opportunities."

"Look what you've become."

"It's got its bad points, but it's got its good points, too. Let's talk inside. I figure the basic color for this play should be blue. During the feast of ghosts half the stage should be raised, and no props. Throughout the scene the actors are in a half crouch, neither kneeling nor standing, since that may be life's most perfect pose. The costumes are white in front, black in back, so when their backs are to the audience there's nothing to see. When the daughter and the college student are talking on the lower half of the stage, a pale, flickering purple light appears above the stage and advances horizontally toward them."

"Then the music starts up," Mu Kun excitedly got into the mood, feeling it was time for each of them to show what they were made of. "We'll use Tan Zhi's composition 'The Palace Tablet,' with a muffled soprano voice repeating the phrase, "Plant melons and harvest melons, plant beans and harvest beans, goodness is rewarded, returning to truth is the only path to pure morals."

"I think Chen Meng's the best choice for the daughter's role," Big Liu said forcefully.

"She's going to do a movie, so the play would come second."

"No, this play's going to be staged in Sweden! Let her play the daughter, and even in her dreams she'd wake up smiling. Yeah, give her the part, and that'll be a real help."

"I don't follow."

"Chen Meng's father is going to be promoted to Deputy Minister of Culture. He's already been interviewed by the people in charge. It's scheduled for the end of the year."

"Really?" Mu Kun was surprised, not by the news itself, but because she was seeing Big Liu with new eyes. She'd always thought that he was content with being a member of the audience where affairs of the world and the ugly dealings among people were concerned, so he could mock them or put on mysterious airs. But

157

now she realized that he was a member of the cast, not the audience, playing a variety of roles earnestly and enthusiastically; he was directing, toying with, and writing the scripts for the various ugly aspects of life. No longer the simple, lovable Big Liu of old. Maybe the stage plans he'd laid out a moment ago were merely meant to get into her good graces. Feeling her heart constrict, she calmly lit a cigarette, took a deep drag, and blew out a thick cloud of smoke, then inhaled it through her nose and blew out another mouthful of pale blue mist.

"That reminds me of a story. A female lab technician spent all her time looking at infected germs and bacteria under her microscope, until she was afraid to touch or eat anything. She starved to death." Her eyes were fixed on Big Liu as she finished her story.

He stared foolishly, uncomprehendingly at her, wondering what the hell kind of medicine she had in her gourd.

Confident that his dull gaze had failed to penetrate her emotional realm, she relished the situation, like a mouse that's encountered a dumb cat. "I'm not going to use Chen Meng, and my reasons are simple: she's not right for the daughter role." She blew out a string of smoke rings, behind which she looked contentedly at the expression on Big Liu's face.

"You'll regret it."

Will I regret it? she asked herself after Big Liu had gone. No, no I won't. No one knew Hua Long better than Mu Kun. Even though he seemed to have born to the middle road and political intrigue, he had devoted his life to becoming a true artist, particularly since becoming president of the academy. He would willingly sacrifice his family and friends, and all his perks to maintain his integrity as an artistic bureaucrat. If she let Chen Meng play the part, everyone would know the reason. Owing to his age, Hua Long wouldn't be allowed to succeed himself as president or be promoted to a higher post. Since one of his sons was studying in England, the other in America, there was no need for him to do anything to compromise his reputation in order to butter up the daughter of the soon-to-be-promoted Deputy Minister of Culture. His ambition — or, more accurately, his obsession — was to wait for the opportune moment to direct a truly contemporary play during the years left to him. He wanted nothing more than to become an internationally renowned director, a world-class artist. Becoming president of the academy had been his freeway to that objective. He had the authority to select the best available play and the finest actors among the teachers and students. And no one would dare quibble with him over expenses.

But for a combination of reasons — government policies and the general state of affairs — his chance still hadn't come. Mu Kun entertained the idea of asking him to be her art director, but quickly changed her mind, knowing *it* would only be a childish attempt at brown-nosing. Five years earlier Hua's production of *Peer Gynt* had been widely praised in theatrical circles in Europe and America, and even though he wouldn't say so, he would consider the adding of his name to a gaudy little nondescript play an insult. For Mu Kun it was essential to contact people whose talent was widely recognized but who were not yet well established, in order to put together a young, vibrant troupe of high quality and low social standing. That would guarantee everyone's sympathy and attention, while any hint of unfairness would surely lead to a suppression of talented youth.

As things stood now, it was essential to use Blackie's translation, since that would elicit plenty of publicity and support by Scandinavian Sinologists. The role of the old man should go to Baohua, an actor who had given up everything for art, including leaving his family and giving up all pleasures; the foolish young man had lived on packaged noodles for over a decade. Neither a star nor a recognized master, he had never won a single acting award; but his performances drew sighs of astonishment. Naturally there was more to it than just an affirmation of his talent and willingness to sacrifice personal pleasures for art; included was a measure of traditional Chinese sympathies for the underdog.

159

One play led to another; ten led to a hundred, until Baohua's performances became the new emperor's clothes. Anyone considering himself a patron of the arts, whether he understood his work or appreciated his performances, sighed emotionally over his pathological attitude toward art. Letting him play the old man in *The Ghost Sonata* would contribute immensely to the success of the play. Mu Kun's actions were always as fast as her thoughts, sometimes even faster. Only when an action presented itself clearly did she begin to give some hazy thought to its causes and effects. Without stopping to finish her noodles, she wanted to talk Baohua one-on-one before Blackie and Big Liu got back to the dorm.

Raising her fist to knock on the door, she heard Baohua and Wu Yun talking in Huang Shizhi's room, and realized that Huang had beaten her to the punch. Then she had an idea. She knocked on the door of room 602 as loudly as possible.

"Who is it? I'm in 601." Baohua opened Huang Shizhi's door and stuck his head out.

"It's me, Mu Kun. I want to talk to you about something. But we can talk in Teacher Huang's room, that's fine." She strode into Huang Shizhi's room. By the messy look of the room and the still slightly flushed cheeks on Huang's ashen face, she guessed that he was driving himself, not getting enough sleep or eating well, because of *Miss Julie,* and that he'd been talking to Baohua and Wu Yun with obvious excitement. Feigning disinterest in what was going on, Mu Kun decided to lay her cards on the table without making it look like an act. "Great," she said casually, "just the two people I was looking for. Baohua, if I can stage *The Ghost Sonata,* I'd like you to play the old man. I don't have to tell you how appealing the role is. And Wu Yun, you can have the daughter role if you want it." Making the second offer was a spur-of-the-moment decision, since Wu Yun happened to be there; another opportunity to undercut Huang Shizhi. Baohua stood there, mouth agape, not knowing what to do, his eyes darting back and forth between Huang Shizhi and Mu Kun. She knew at once that her initial assumption had been right on target.

160

Wu Yun squinted and smiled innocently, giving nothing away. She had quickly evaluated the situation and made a quick judgment regarding the antagonists' power and prospects, including, of course, their comparative talents as directors. At first, Mu Kun hadn't placed much importance on her attitude toward playing the daughter's role, but now that the little witch was trying a balancing act she was infuriated. She'd force her to swallow the bait, or else. Obsessed with winning, she acted accordingly, by revealing her lineup: Blackie's translated script, the Swedish student Christopher's plans for form, Big Liu's stagecraft, Baohua as the old man, and, if Wu Yun had a problem, then Chen Meng as the daughter...

Blackie's translated script? Christopher's plans for form? Wu Yun stood up and her tiny eyes, suddenly big and round, seemed to light up.

Seeing her excitement, Huang Shizhi knew that this news would make the rounds at the academy the next morning.

Mu Kun, having gotten what she wanted, asked patronizingly:

"Well, what do you two think?"

Baohua was already caught up in the role of the old man, and his choice had never been in doubt. But he didn't enjoy seeing Huang Shizhi completely deflated; so after a moment's reflection, he assumed the expression of a man doing something he knew was wrong, and said stiffly, "That's an intriguing offer. Fortunately I haven't committed myself to doing Jean for Teacher Huang."

Huang Shizhi looked dully at Baohua, who said with his head bowed, "I have to go."

Wu Yun walked up to Mu Kun, rested her hand on her left arm, and said softly, "Your room. We need to talk."

"About what?" Huang Shizhi burst in angrily.

Unmoved by the outburst, Wu Yun flashed Huang a warm smile and said softly, "It's between us girls, nothing you'd know about." Then, like a little angel, she gave him one last innocent smile, took Mu Kun's hand, and fluttered her eyelids. Mu Kun knew she was trying to keep a foot in each boat, so as not to be left out no matter which play was staged. But she reacted to this ineffective little ploy with grand airs, for she was determined to make her attitude clear to Huang Shizhi:

"Since you're willing to play the part, it's all settled."

The blood drained from Huang Shizhi's face, his flushed cheeks now only a memory. If he'd decided to castigate her for trying to ruin him, she'd have taken the rebuke in silence. But she knew he was incapable of this sort of bluntness, and that he lacked the courage to let on that he was unhappy. She smiled magnanimously and patted him on the shoulder. "Teacher Huang, instead of competing, openly or not, why not combine forces? As long as you feel we can coexist, you can sign on as art director for my play. Think it over, would you?"

Huang Shizhi was, after all, a man in his fifties, and thoughts and ideas, as well as the words to express them, always came a beat more slowly to him than to Mu Kun; when he was tense, that went to a beat and a half. Before he'd even figured out her first gambit, he was confronted by a second. As the heat was turned up inside his skull, he warned himself: Forget it, don't try to figure it out. Nothing good will come from engaging this enemy. Taking the rigid line, he declined it all, her good intentions and bad, her magnanimity and consent. By doing nothing he saved her the trouble of opening her bag of tricks. Before he had a chance to completely recover, she walked out, leaving Wu Yun behind and feeling quite pleased with herself.

Chapter 5

The small conference room of the experimental drama troupe seemed about to explode from the mood of depression. Hua Long sat facing a silent group of academic committee members, their minds drifting aimlessly. After listening to Huang Shizhi and Mu Kun report on their directing plans and personnel selections, he waited anxiously for the old-timers to pass on their ruling. But when they rose to speak, they were so ambiguous he wasn't sure how they felt. As always, they were passing the buck up to the next level. Hua Long sat pensively, holding his teacup in both hands. When he glanced over at Mu Kun he saw a look of self-confidence as she took his measure. The sharpness of her gaze was like a dagger piercing his heart. He stirred, as though suddenly invigorated, and had to admit that her personality and her happy-go-lucky lifestyle had more appeal than her feminine exterior. Her keen ambition and single-minded determination to fight until the battle was won, her ability to overpower adversaries, and her knack for avoiding minor squabbles, were qualities that Huang Shizhi, an intellectual worn down by political hardships, lacked.

Even though the play Mu Kun wanted to direct was showy and turbulent, it lacked deep artistic appeal and profound cultural relevance. But she was only thirty years old, after all! And she was capable of flashes of brilliant emotion. If these flecks of gold and shards of jade could somehow be fused together, they might create an artistic treasure. She was an artistic embryo waiting for the right moment, the right circumstances, and the right signs to be born. If, at her energetic and emotional peak, she was given the right training, a broader outlook, and the right opportunity, she might become a true artist, which could fundamentally change her life... it suddenly occurred to Hua Long that he had been gazing at Mu Kun too long, which might give the committee the mistaken impression that he favored her.

With a glance at the expressions around the table, he shifted his gaze to the ashen face of Huang Shizhi, someone he saw as a dedicated lover of dramatic art who had endured half a lifetime of trials and tribulations in theatrical circles. He was a man of passion and an impressive cultural background who somehow had never gained an understanding of the soul of art. His directing skills surpassed those of his peers, for he had the ability to probe the unknown depths of his actors' untapped feelings. Based upon his years of stage experience and his technical skills, he was capable of staging a performance of *Miss Julie* that would earn the festival critics' accolades. But it was beyond his ability to create something unique, to amaze his audience, or to invest his script with new meaning or vitality.

As for Mu Kun, even though it was a sort of game with her, she could play it for all it was worth, and show what she was made of. Her play would undoubtedly spark debate between her supporters and detractors, depending upon their personal tastes. If they liked it, she would win hands down; if not, they would leave with an unbearably bad taste in their mouths.

"Old Huang, Little Mu, we'd like to hear what you think. Be frank." Sensing that the chill had lasted too long, Hua Long opened up a new avenue.

"I don't think it's my place to do that. I'll go along with whatever you decide."

"How about you, little Mu?" Hua Long asked off-handedly.

"Naturally I hope you gentlemen will give me a chance to participate in the drama festival. As far as I'm concerned, *The Ghost Sonata* offers more opportunities for a director than *Miss Julie*. And the troupe I've put together is better. In terms of concepts and intent, mine's more original and unconventional than Teacher Huang's, without being superficial...

164

The members of the academic committee stirred. Huang Shizhi looked scornfully at Mu Kun, disgusted by her comments, although he experienced a faint sense of contentment, and began to hope she'd say something even more arrogant, even more barefaced, for that would surely spark feelings of disgust among the old-timers sitting around the table.

"I know that what I've said must strike you as arrogant and immodest. But that's the way I feel. Candor is part of my personality and a rule I live by. You can view it as a flaw if you'd like, or as a commendable quality. Teacher Huang and I are adversaries in this, and I'm sure he wants to win, too. It's just that he's more reserved and won't admit it." She thus preempted the old-timers' discussion of her earlier comments, and gave the impression of youthful innocence and likability. Her goal achieved, she smiled confidently at Huang Shizhi, who kept his anger and jealous loathing in check in the presence of a roomful of his superiors, and grinned awkwardly to show magnanimity toward his younger colleague.

"All right, now that you've described your plans and ideas, I'll ask you to step outside and continue your preparations while we deliberate. You'll have our decision after winter vacation," Hua Long announced in the tone of someone seeking approbation.

"Fine, fine," Huang said compliantly as he stood up, a bit too quickly; he saw a flurry of stars in front of his eyes. He stumbled, steadied himself by leaning against the wall, and stood for a moment with his eyes closed.

"What's wrong?" several of the old-timers asked anxiously.

Mu Kun rushed over to help. "Burning too much midnight oil, Venerable Huang?"

He pushed her hand away disgustedly. "It's nothing. I sat there too long, and my foot went to sleep." He let his gaze sweep the roomful of white-haired old men and said meaningfully, "Now I'm Venerable Huang in her eyes." Thrusting out his chest and raising his head in a show of youthful vigor, he headed out of the room, as the discussion got underway.

"Why hasn't the situation with his wife been settled yet?"

"We've sent up two requests, but they've both been denied. Since she's a worker we can't manage the exchange."

"If I'm not mistaken, she's been here for some time now..."

The discussion behind him filled Huang Shizhi with mixed feelings of gratitude and sadness, for he knew that the sympathy of these powerless old scholars counted for absolutely nothing. As he walked into the block of flats he felt sharp pains in his abdomen, and had to go to the bathroom so badly he shivered. Keeping one hand on the bannister, he held his belly with the other. More sharp pains doubled him up as he / rushed toward the toilet. When he finished he could barely stand up, and the sight of bloody stool drained him of nearly all his remaining strength. He stumbled and walked out of the toilet, managing to climb to the sixth floor, where he entered his room with faltering steps and collapsed weakly onto the bed.

"What's wrong? Did they turn you down?" his tiny wife was sitting in a chair, her feet not touching the floor, like an aging child.

Huang lay there without moving, as though lifeless. After a moment he moaned and said, "Get one of those forms out of the drawer. I need to go see a doctor."

"What's wrong?" She jumped out of her chair, like a little knockdown doll, and walked up to the bed, where she took his ice-cold hand in hers.

"I had blood in my stool." His voice sounded like a puddle of sticky blood.

Not daring to pursue the matter, his wife took a form out of the drawer and helped him to his feet.

166

"If anybody asks, tell them I've got a cold," he said repeatedly as they walked out the door. "Say nothing, okay?"

She looked at him uncomprehendingly, but even though his secret was beyond her, she nodded to make him feel better.

The hospital of traditional medicine. Huang Shizhi and his wife squeezed in among a sea of gray, gaunt faces. After registering as an emergency patient he sat in a cold, whistling north wind for half an hour, before finally being seated stiffly beside the desk of a young female doctor, who asked him a few questions about his medical history and gave him a perfunctory examination. "Why'd you wait so long?" she asked reproachfully. Huang's heart leapt into his throat and seemed to want to stay there. He kept sizing up the doctor, and from the look on her face when she handed the lab test form to his wife, he had a premonition that things were looking pretty bad.

When she sent him back to the waiting room to rest, he sensed a fearful end just around the corner. I can't die now! My wife's health is fragile, and even though I'm in my fifties, we have to live apart. Our son's about to graduate from high school, and the quality of education in his rural school is so bad that if I can't bring him to Beijing to complete his studies his future is ruined. There's so much to do. I can't die now and leave a widow and child behind... His sense of responsibility darkened his mood even more. He stood up, took a turn around the waiting room, then sat back down, with a single thought in his mind: Going to Sweden could be the glimmer of hope my son needs... He couldn't get that off his mind, and his thoughts kept taking the tortuous path toward the drama festival. His wife walked up with a downcast expression on her face, not daring to look up. She'd been crying, he assumed, maybe was still crying inside. His heart felt hot and dry; once he lost control he rushed into the doctor's office.

"What is it?" she asked without looking up from the chart she was writing on.

"Is it cancer?"

"No. I told your wife we wouldn't have the results of the smear test for three days. I can tell you what's wrong then. I want you to take it easy for a few days."

"It can't be cancer!" He stepped forward excitedly, grabbed her sleeve, and asked earnestly, "Is it cancer or not? I have to know the truth."

"I'll tell you one more time. It's not, but we still don't know what's wrong.

"Don't try to pacify me, I can take it."

"Okay, if you say it is, then it is. Now please go outside. I have other patients to see."

"It can't be cancer, it can't! It doesn't feel like it!" Huang's feelings were confused. He doubted his own doubts, but he also doubted the doctor's denial.

"You're too excitable. Get some rest." Her patience gone, she called in the next patient, and ignored Huang's questions.

When his wife returned, he grabbed her hand. "It can't be cancer," he said, for his own benefit as well as for hers.

"It can't be cancer," she echoed him, pulling a long face.

Huang Shizhi stood in the doorway looking panic-stricken at the chaotic scene in the patient-filled hospital. After a moment he mumbled, "If it is, and I need surgery, I won't do it here."

"Why not?"

"I can't let the people at the academy know I'm sick..."

"Don't think so much..."

"I've let you and our son down, but even if I die tomorrow I'll make sure you're taken care of." Having already assumed the role of a cancer victim, he was feeling his responsibilities as a husband and a father more keenly than ever.

"You don't have what you're talking about."

"Even if I do I have to stage that play! When I get overseas I'll arrange things for our son, and you'll be taken care of in your later years."

His tiny wife hadn't realized he was capable of such fond feelings, such tenderness. She buried her head in his chest and sobbed.

Seeing her curled up, her head buried in his chest, so frail and pitiful, seemed to invest him with a sacred mission, and his mood began to stabilize, his determination grew. Stroking her head, he consoled her, "Don't cry, calm down. We'll think of something."

She looked up at him pitifully, like people in a liberated area gaze up at the Big Dipper.

"We can go to the Anhui Malignant Tumor Hospital."

"How can their skills compare with Beijing?"

"If I'm in a Beijing hospital we won't be able to keep it quiet. The head of surgery there is an old friend. That settles it. Now let's dry our eyes and go home." He helped her up and they left the hospital with gloomy looks on their faces. They climbed the stairs to their flat.

"Well, did you go to the hospital?" Mu Kun asked the exhausted Huang Shizhi when they met on the fifth floor.

"Nonsense, why would I go to the hospital? I was out taking a walk with my wife." He squeezed his wife's hand as a sign to keep their secret. Under such strange circumstances he both hated and feared Mu Kun, while she was moved by his tenderness toward his wife. He hadn't abandoned this tiny woman who looked like a dwarf, even if she wasn't one, after all these years, and to Mu Kun this was pretty terrific. After being the object of emotional assaults and romantic games by so many lovely girls, he must be pretty special to resist such temptations, irrespective of morality, assuming he hadn't lost all desire and feeling. The obvious mutual affection between this aging Romeo and Juliet moved Mu Kun like a little hand tearing gently at the scars in her heart, producing suffering that went beyond mere pain. Her nose ached and a dampness settled over her heart; compassion slowly covered the bleeding scars. No more competing. Maybe going abroad will be the catalyst that brings this aging couple together again, she was thinking.

A nameless anger welled up in Huang Shizhi as Mu Kun kept gazing at him. But the strong feminine odor of a healthy, mature woman emanating from her was so overwhelming he could barely breathe. This contrast and Mu Kun's condescending concern were more than he could bear. Jealous loathing overcame his magnanimity; despair gave birth to malice.

"What's that, a letter from across the Pacific?" He could see that the letter in her hand had a domestic stamp on it, but asked anyway.

"No."

"He must be doing pretty well these days."

"Money's a problem. He has to work *and* study."

"You must be mistaken. Didn't Zeng Li see him in Hawaii on vacation with a friend?"

Mu Kun detected the malignant intent in his comment. Her husband's classmate had seen him on vacation in Hawaii with the girl during the summer. But she kept her anger in check and said unaffectedly, "Oh, he went there with some rich girl so he wouldn't have use his own money. Men away from their women are like fish out of water. Except for workaholics like you, of course."

"Well, you're certainly open-minded."

Mu Kun smiled indifferently and slipped back into her room.

As he watched her lively silhouette, what seemed like two rows of razor-sharp teeth surfaced in Huang's heart and began biting down painfully. He had to beat her, he just had to. He couldn't allow a mere child like that to destroy his prestige. Returning to his room with no thoughts of resting, he picked up his Swedish textbook to go to class.

"Have you lost your mind?" his wife blurted out as she stood in his way.

"I'm better than her, even in Swedish!" Huang Shizhi gazed out the window over his wife's head.

"Are you willing to throw your life away?"

"Yes, if necessary! Now get out of my way, I'm late!" He strode majestically out of the room, like an invincible warrior. Many thoughts accompanied him on his way, including what it would be like when his wife saw him off at the airport and how dejected Mu Kun would be after her defeat. He was feeling a little better now. But when he recalled the arrogant expression on Mu Kun's face and her wildly presumptuous comments, his anger was nearly suffocating. Struggles these days are so frightening, young people today are so frightening, each generation is more frightening than the one before. These thoughts reminded him that he was getting old, that the world was leaving him behind.

He thought back to the first day of Swedish class. He was ten minutes late. Instead of walking right in, he stood outside the door to compose himself, then swaggered into the room, only to be thrown into uncontrollable embarrassment by the stares of the youngsters filling the seats. It was as though he'd crawled out of a crypt. The world was no longer his, and that saddened him. The advertisement had said only that classes met on Monday, Wednesday, and Friday nights, at a cost of thirty-five yuan a month; nowhere had it stipulated an age requirement. Who cared if you were a child or an adult, as long as you paid up? Quickly regaining control of his mood, Huang nodded politely to the female instructor, who directed him to a seat in the last row. Once seated, he took out his textbook, a notebook, and a pen, then put on his reading glasses and stared at the instructor without so much as blinking.

His gaze so embarrassed her that she averted her eyes as she said genially to the youngsters in the classroom, "Since it's our first day, I'd like to start by hearing why you're here and what you expect. That will help me meet your needs in this course..." She stepped down from the podium and stood next to a girl of fourteen or fifteen. "Do you have a background in Swedish?" she asked pleasantly. "Why do you want to study it?"

The girl flicked her short hair and said confidently, "I know some simple conversation. My father speaks Swedish. He's lecturing in Stockholm, and next spring I'll be going to school there."

"How about you?"

A boy with a small nose and tiny eyes stood up and hemmed and hawed for a moment without saying much of anything. The only thing Huang Shizhi could make out was that his elder sister's boyfriend was a self-supporting student in Sweden.

"And you?"

"My uncle went on a fact-finding mission to Scandinavia last year, and he said that even though Sweden's a small country, it has a

172

terrific social welfare system. My mom asked someone in the Western Languages Department at Peking University, who told her that hardly anybody studies Swedish, not like English, where the number of students is frightening. So I chose Swedish. That way I won't have to compete with so many people."

"And you?"

"My mom has patients in the Swedish Embassy. She practices traditional medicine, and a lot of her Swedish friends want to help her get to Sweden."

"My dad's novel has been translated into Swedish, and the royalties will be enough for me to study for a year."

"My sister-in-law has performed in a Swedish opera house..."

"My brother taught Chinese to two Swedish students..."

My God! Huang Shizhi was shocked to see that in such a small class there were so many people who had their hearts set on Sweden; and so many connections, visible and otherwise. Can people really be that mercenary? Has China really embarked on a naked struggle for capitalist accumulations? Mu Kun's generation is nothing compared to this group of youngsters! In the midst of his shock and emotional dejection, he burst out laughing when he heard the response of one of the boys.

"We live in a tiny room, and my brother doesn't want me around when he's with his girlfriend. So he paid sixty yuan for me to take this class. I have to be here on Mondays, Wednesdays, and Fridays *and* on Tuesdays, Thursdays, and Saturdays. I don't even have time to do my winter vacation homework."

The instructor tactfully quieted the laughing students down, then said softly, "Now that you've all had a chance to introduce yourselves, I know why you're here and what you need." She nodded politely to Huang Shizhi to let him know he didn't need to say anything in front of the children. It was a sign of respect. He smiled to show his gratitude.

The instructor spent the first session introducing the twenty-nine letters of the Swedish alphabet, and the second asking each student to stand up and recite them. Before his turn came around, Huang Shizhi began writing Chinese phonetics beside the letters to help him pronounce them; he didn't want to make a fool of himself in front of all those children. But in his nervousness, he couldn't find an appropriate phonetic for some of them, no matter how he racked his brain. When the girl in front of him stood up for her turn, he thought his heart would leap out of his chest. He laid down his pen and closed his eyes, forcing himself not to think of any of the letters, preferring to wait until it was his turn to stand up and see what happened. When the girl finished her recitation, without a single mistake, Huang nearly stood up by reflex. But the instructor walked gently past him and stood next to a boy in the back row.

Even after several weeks, the memory of this session was still clearly etched in his mind. Although the instructor was treating him respectfully, he'd missed the chance to have his pronunciation corrected, and every time she corrected one of the children he derided himself for his vanity and pettiness. Was he, an old man, spending all this time and money for a pitiful bit of self-respect in front of the children? Time and again he felt like asking the instructor to let him change seats, since his chronic insomnia had led to a ringing in his ears and made it difficult to see the board; but for some reason he never opened his mouth. Then one day he entered the classroom first and, without a second thought, took a seat in the front row, right in the center. When the little princess saw him in her desk with a stern look on his face she stuck up her nose, gave him a nasty "hmph" look, and took another seat.

The instructor, who either didn't notice or didn't seem to care that Huang had changed seats, smiled and nodded warmly, as always, and began the day's work. Before introducing the new lesson she always had the students recite the previous lesson; but she never called on him. Today he was feeling generally angry, sure that he'd become an outcast, like a husk in a bowl of rice you spit out. It was as though his feelings and emotions, his every action, had nothing to do with anyone else; he was sick of this cold-shoulder treatment, this unbearable neglect. Raising his head, he looked around searchingly, and the sight of all those raised hands lit a nameless fire inside him. As one of the students finished his recitation, Huang's pudgy, ashen hand shot up. After a momentary shock, the instructor said politely, "All right, let's have Teacher Huang recite the previous lesson. You needn't stand, you can recite from your desk."

The children's curious glances and the instructor's respectful attitude took the edge off his anger, but increased the pressure. He cleared his throat and tried to breathe normally. But his voice wasn't up to the effort and cracked at its first attempt. The children buzzed, whispered to each other, and made faces. Then they burst out laughing. But he kept a stern look on his face as he looked at the hilarious antics of the children and sat there in rigid silence. The net effect of his wooden, muted appearance, which made him look slow-witted, was uncontrollable laughter. Tiny drops of perspiration dotted his brow, each containing the shimmering glare of a cold light. He dug his fingernails into the palms of his hands and rolled his textbook into a tight little wand. He grew tense, his muscles tautened, and he smacked the top of his desk with the rolled-up book. "Stop laughing!" he bellowed, without a quiver in his voice.

This unexpected outburst brought immediate silence. The children lowered their heads, not daring to look at the standing Huang Shizhi.

"I don't have time to prepare my lessons. I have my own classes to prepare, and I'm working on a stage play, which means finding actors and working out the plot. I have to cook, do the laundry, stand in line to buy kerosene, run around trying to get my son accepted in a correspondence school, and go out every day to read notices for job-swaps tacked up on telephone poles..." He was so wrought up he couldn't go on. Picking up his book, he slowly read the day's lesson. The classroom was absolutely still, as looks of seriousness spread across the children's' faces, whose ears were pricked as they listened to stuff that wasn't in the lesson. When Huang finished he slumped down into the little desk as though his body had come unglued. After a long, silent moment the instructor walked up next to him and said softly, "Teacher Huang, why don't you go home." He raised his head and looked at her, his eyes puffy, without saying a word.

"I saw your production of *Hell Screen* when I was a little girl. I loved it." Her voice was as soft and delicate as a strand of silk floating gently down to Huang's ear. He snapped his eyes shut, stood up and walked solemnly out of the classroom. A large hazy shadow moved unsteadily across the snow-white wall.

Chapter 6

The patter of fine rain mixed with snowflakes seemed never ending. The people's hearts were distended and mildewed by the dampness. Just before winter break Huang Shizhi suddenly asked for a leave of absence to attend to his aging father's serious illness, and left Beijing in a hurry. Then a few days before the new semester he reappeared on campus, his face unusually gaunt and ashen, although he was still excitable, like an insomniac on a caffeine high after too many cups of strong coffee. He stuck out his chest and held his head high, too exaggerated to look normal; his legs seemed to drag as he walked, apparently unable to keep pace with his desire. People guessed that he was lying low while Mu Kun was active on all fronts. But others suspected that he'd gone south to make a TV movie for some foreign currency, without having to give the academy its cut. Only Mu Kun had an inkling of what was going on with him. Even though she knew the views of the academic committee, and was privy to Hua Long's final decision, since it hadn't been made public, it was like a balloon perched above a pin, which could pop at any minute. The more she pondered Huang's unusual behavior the more uncomfortable she felt.

"Oh, you're back! Is your father better?" she asked amiably when they met on his second day back.

"Much better!" There was a husky quality to Huang's voice, as though he wanted the whole world to hear him.

"Isn't it pretty late to be going out in this weather?"

"I'm going to ask Hua *xiansheng* where things stand. I want to know which play has been approved." He seemed like a different man, stoic and straightforward. She could hardly believe her ears.

"It, uh, hasn't been made public," she replied without her usual glibness, intimidated by his manner.

177

"Come back here," his wife rushed out to say. "You haven't eaten yet..." Her words trailed off when she saw Mu Kun.

Huang glared reproachfully at his wife, then, with a look of suspicion in his eyes, glanced vacantly and meaninglessly at Mu Kun before turning and walking out.

All the unusual signs she'd gotten from Huang planted doubts in Mu Kun's mind. Of course she could think of a hundred reasons why Hua Long wouldn't change his mind, but she couldn't shake the image of the balloon perched above the pin, worrying that Huang Shizhi might just move it enough for it to pop. In order to ask the opinions of as many people as possible, she went to Blackie's and knocked on his door, without even stopping to eat. Steam from a mutton fire-pot filled the room, and as Mu Kun stepped inside she was greeted by waves of fragrance. Seated around the table, enveloped by the steam, were seven or eight men facing two twelve-wick lanterns, eating like there was no tomorrow.

"Ah, Director Mu, join us. We're out of stools, but it goes down faster if you stand, anyway." Big Liu handed her a pair of chopsticks and a glass of beer.

"What's the happy event? Whose treat?"

Baohua was digging in so spiritedly his face was covered with grease. He pointed to Big Liu without pausing.

Big Liu smugly and boorishly patted the back of the young man sitting next to him. He was wearing a Western suit, but looked very stiff. "We were kids together. He leaves tomorrow to study in Australia."

"Oh!" Mu Kun's gaze and the expression on her face made the young man squirm uncomfortably. He raised his glass, and even though it covered the lower half of his face, it couldn't cover the lack of self-confidence in his eyes.

"My buddy here is tired of business dealings, so he bribed the general manager of a Danish electrical equipment company to send him an employment contract. The salary was kept low to reduce the percentage that had to be paid to the China Labor Corporation, only US$600 for six months. It worked. Tomorrow he'll be on a plane bound for capitalism!" Big Liu turned and slapped the shoulder of another young man next to him whose hair and clothes gave him an effeminate look. His smile disappeared as quickly as the foam on a glass of beer.

Possibly because the joy of success had suddenly settled over the first young man, he tried to look complacent, but had trouble making his expression believable.

"Can you speak Danish?" Mu Kun asked artlessly, her gaze sweeping his face a couple of times.

"I can barely speak Chinese, let alone Danish!" he said, jamming his hand into the pocket of his red trousers, hoping that his words and actions showed what a clever young modern he was.

"If I could why would I need to go study it?" He felt obligated to answer her, his first comment having met with a chilly silence.

"You're going there to study? Didn't you say you were given an employment contract?"

"He's spending his own money and just using the company's name," Big Liu answered for his friend. "That was to take care of the China Labor Corporation fee. And it was a good deal for the general manager, since my buddy has agreed not to contact the company when he gets there, no matter what happens."

"I'll work while I go to school. In a social welfare country it's easy to make enough to get by, including housing and a car." He

179

spoke with the affected nasal quality of foreigners, snorting complacently.

As Mu Kun listened to him talk about how Chinese make their fortunes abroad, from teaching breathing exercises to becoming masseurs and chefs, she had the feeling that he was going abroad with his eyes closed, and that even though his future was in doubt, he was blindly confident in his abilities. In contrast, she knew she was long past the stage in her life where a sense of adventure and an ability to indulge in fantasies existed.

Blackie walked into the room smoking a cigar when the party was in full swing. His clouded face seemed bundled in snow and mist. Skirting the table, he sat down at his desk without so much as looking at the steaming pot, not saying a word.

"Come over and dig in," Baohua and a couple of the guests said politely.

Big Liu waved his chopsticks and said, "Forget it, leave him alone with his thoughts for a moment. Food for the soul is a lot more important than common mutton."

On the other side of the steam that separated him from the others, Blackie's look was glum and scary.

"What's wrong now?" Mu Kun said as she walked up cautiously.

"I think..." Blackie puffed deeply on his cigar, then closed his mouth tightly and didn't go on. It looked like he might not finish his sentence until next year. Mu Kim, on pins and needles waiting to hear what he had to say, kept her eyes on his mouth. Finally, as ribbons of blue smoke emerged from the nostrils of his large, flat nose, he continued his thought, "I think your play's been assassinated."

"Why?" Mu Kun's heart skipped a beat and her skin tensed.

"Because you're using my translated script."

Suddenly he was a mystery, body and soul, to her. All the dangers she had feared were now embodied in the dramatic aspects of his personality.

Blackie blew out a cloud of cloud and closed his eyes again, pensively. As he snubbed out the half-smoked cigar he muttered, "Maybe it's for the best! Assassinating my script will only spark an even stronger reaction among our foreign friends. They'll see how China's authorities suppress talent and recognize their ugly conduct where art is concerned! We're going to have to prepare ourselves mentally..."

"Ah---" Blackie's gloomy mood drew a long sigh of relief from Mu Kun. But her heart had no sooner calmed down than it was struck by an even more ominous thought:

Was this just a trick by Blackie, killing the production of *The Ghost Sonata* in order to cause a political incident? In modern-day China the more strongly a work of art is attacked, especially if it's banned, the more favorable attention it draws, the publicity increasing the stature of its author. But gaining notoriety from criticism wasn't her road to success, and certainly not the goal she'd set for herself. It was essential that she has a chance to display her talents as a director; she needed to direct, and she needed the emotional boost of the audience's excited response. She wanted to raise her stature, but only through the play. There was danger lurking, and her only protection was to go see Hua Long and get everything out into the open; that might spur him into making his final decision.

"That's right, we're going to have to prepare ourselves mentally." She walked back to the table, but the mutton had lost its appeal. Blackie's comments were like a jagged rock stuck in her chest. But as the head of a drama troupe she needed to appear steady and magnanimous, so she acted as though nothing Blackie said had affected her, in order to keep the others from growing restless.

181

"Don't get bent out of shape over stuff like that, okay?" Big Liu, starting to feel depressed, said as he threw down his chopsticks.

Blackie kept his eyes closed as a pose.

"Go ahead and stuff your buddies into your political pocket for your own sake, and to hell with us nobodies! But if you do, I'll publicly withdraw from the troupe, because I'm not about to jeopardize my chances of getting a passport for Australia!"

"Don't turn tail and run away before you even see danger." Mu Kun looked at Big Liu as though he were a slimy creature.

"I'm not chicken shit! But if you're going to be a hero make sure it's worth it!"

The greasy mouths around the table stopped moving, and the only sound in the room was the water boiling in the fire-pot. Mu Kun sensed that the conversation had taken a bad turn, and that if something wasn't done fast, Blackie's off-hand comment could ruin everything. Not wanting to say anything more, she slipped out while everyone sat there glumly, then ran to Hua Long's home, realizing when she got there that she'd made another galling mistake: not only hadn't she thought the issue out clearly, but she had no idea how she was going to make sure Hua Long knew what Blackie was up to without suspecting that she was betraying a friend. She hesitated for a moment, trying to decide whether she should leave or stay, when the sound of the door opening nearly made her jump in alarm.

"Who is it?" Huang Shizhi stepped back timidly and turned on the porch light. "Oh, it's you!" He stared at her, unable to say a word, as he looked daggers at her, which passed right through her head.

Mu Kun, caught off guard, avoided his eyes; about to explain why she was there, she realized it would be a waste of time, no matter what she said; so she said nothing. Think what you want to think!

"Oh, it's little Mu. You can see yourself out, can't you, Shizhi?" In a move to lighten the atmosphere, Hua Long casually patted them both on the shoulder.

Huang Shizhi gathered in his gaze, feeling a ringing in his large, empty skull. The tiring trip, the excitement of talking with Hua Long about the play, and the shock of seeing Mu Kun combined to sap his remaining energy. Lacking the strength to move his legs, he slumped to the side. He wanted to rest against the bannister to catch his breath, but when he saw that Hua Long and Mu Kun were watching him he raised his head, threw out his chest, and took a step with his right foot. The porch light went out, and in the blackness the only light came from the stars in front of his eyes. He stepped down, missed the step, and fell hard on the stairs, knocking what seemed like a plastic pail crashing down to the landing. Hua Long flipped on the porch light as Mu Kun went out to help Huang Shizhi up. But he scrambled to his feet with amazing speed and leaned lightly up against the bannister. His face was clouded and expressionless. Although he was looking at Hua Long, he didn't seem to see him. A foul-smelling, sticky substance oozed from a cream-colored rubber tube down his leg and dripped onto the stairs. He grabbed the synthetic drip tube under his shirt and closed his eyes weakly.

"Teacher Huang, you..."

Like a man awakening from a dream, Huang said, "I had it done when I was away..."

"Don't say anything." Mu Kun's heart constricted as it filled with sorrow and pity. She felt as cold as if she'd been immersed in frost and snow. She retrieved his plastic waste bottle, then watched him reattach it to the rubber tube as warm tears formed in the corners of her eyes. She wanted to comfort him and let him know how she felt, but before she could get the words out, another emotion grabbed her and wouldn't let go: If she didn't back up her words with action, anything she said would be pure hypocrisy.

"Really, I didn't..." Huang wanted to explain himself, but before the words were out, even he felt it would be a waste of time.

Hua Long had been standing there with his head lowered all this time, staring at the tips of his shoes without saying anything.

Huang steadied himself after a moment, dusted himself off, politely refused Hua Long and Mu Kun's offer to see him home, and walked down the stairs, his feet seemingly floating, his body swaying, like an old man who'd had the marrow of his bones sucked dry; he stumbled along like a candle flickering in the wind. The world of colors had been reduced to cinders in his heart.

"I'd better be leaving, too," Mu Kun said softly, like a moist floating mist, to keep from startling Hua Long.

"I want to talk to you," he said, putting his arm around her shoulder, as though she were his own daughter, and steering her into his living room, where he poured her a glass of juice and peeled an apple. He even opened a box of fine chocolates before sitting in the sofa across from her and studying her face. Mu Kun accepted his gaze without losing her composure. She had a vague idea of what he was about to say, and was ready for it. He kept tapping his forehead with his finger, and his eyes were filled with a look of embarrassment. She had a perfect read of what he was going to say, and why.

From the moment he'd seen Huang Shizhi's synthetic drip-tube a decision had begun to form in his mind. Now it was just a matter of convincing her and figuring out how to make things up to her and to her troupe. What was the best way to get the members of her troupe to accept his decision calmly? He didn't want to do anything to hurt this lively, lovely young director, his daughter (by now he was seeing her as his own daughter). Nor did he want to use his authority or some underhanded means to extinguish the rays of hope that filled her heart. More than anything he wanted her to do the job she was capable of doing. He wanted to see a lovable little seedling take root and grow gracefully in the rich, abundant soil he

184

had to offer, someday growing into a towering tree, even if its lush branches and leaves covered him and the ground at his feet.

But Huang Shizhi needed his help more, for he'd paid a far more grievous price to realize his goal. He might not be able to survive the severing of this last thread of hope. And if that happened, his feelings of grief and unfairness would echo throughout the academy. Hua Long was not about to be the cause of such a tragedy, nor do anything in the waning days of his tenure as president that would leave the impression of an unfeeling bureaucrat. What to do? He could think of no way to make this up to Huang Shizhi, and was powerless to arrange for the transfer of Huang's wife to Beijing. Sacrificing Mu Kun's chance was the only way he'd ever be able compensate Huang for a lifetime of misfortune. But that still didn't make it fair, not where Mu Kun was concerned..., no, she's still young, and he'd make it up to her somehow. Even if I'm not the president, I'll do everything in my power to help her stage a play and go abroad... gradually, his guilt was replaced by feelings of fatherly love and responsibility. With the appropriate look on his face, he let his gaze wander gently over her face as he said softly, "This is probably Huang Shizhi's last chance..."

"Don't say it." She lowered her head so he wouldn't see the tears glistening in her eyes. Since her hands were trembling slightly, she steadied them by thrusting them under her legs until they began to ache and turn numb. This was the closest she'd ever been to Hua Long's heart, and now she understood his character as never before. He was a kindly grandfather who placed great importance on establishing that image in the presence of his grandchildren, someone who wanted to hold the bowl even to share his love equally among all the children and keep them from harm. He was also an artist who was often overcome by his emotions beneath a veneer of middle-of-the-road rationality and political acumen. Sometimes he appeared circumspect and astute, at other times totally ineffectual; he was capable of tearing down one wall to repair another when faced with chaos and dilapidation, at an incredible waste of materials and manpower.

185

Seeing Mu Kun engrossed in her thoughts, Hua Long assumed that her competitiveness had been won over by feelings of sympathy; a smile as fresh as a pool of spring water spread across his face, as if he'd been relieved of a heavy burden. Moved by her good sense and altruism, he wanted to pay her tribute, but as soon as the words were out, even he felt they sounded officious and grating: "Little Mu, you're young, talented, and healthy. You have a bright future ahead of you…" He was shocked by how the title "president" made dissimulation so easy, and his thoughts went in different directions. He didn't know what else to say.

"Since I'm young and talented, not to mention healthy, that means I'm more qualified and have more stamina to engage in international competition than Teacher *Huang!* If I had money I'd invest it in charitable works. But where life and work are concerned, I can't abandon what I have just because my opponent stumbles and falls. I don't have the right to throw away this opportunity. If I did, not only would I let myself down, but the troupe as well. If you exercise your authority in this case, we'll fight you to the end." Her voice was determined yet calm as she looked straight into Hua Long's confused, dispirited eyes.

"I wish you'd understand my…"

"Hua *xiansheng,* I've never understood you, or respected you, more than I do at this moment. That's why I'm talking to you as if you were my peer. I want you to understand me…"

Hua Long stood up straight, the dispirited look in his eyes disappearing as he observed Mu Kim. Her face looked like a breath of spring, magnanimous, natural, and genuine. She was like a glittering transparent body, with her attributes and flaws, her goals and ambitions, out there for all to see. Her youth and the splendid aspects of her body filled him with love; but of course her indomitable spirit frightened …

In Hua Long's face Mu Kun saw old age, affection, and a primitive tolerance. She understood him, but she couldn't do his

186

bidding. She didn't want to hurt him, but that's exactly what she was doing. Being in his presence depressed her, so she steeled herself, cleared her mind of confusing thoughts, and ran outside to fill her lungs with clean, fresh air, before quickly vanishing into the misty night.

ABOUT THE AUTHOR

Ai Bei is from Beijing, China. After her graduation from a medical school, she was teaching and practicing medicine at a hospital associated with the school. She has published more than two-dozen short stories and six novels in Mainland China, Taiwan, Hong Kong, Malaysia, United States and other countries.

Her novels are noted for perceiving the deep structure of humanity from the ordinary perspectives of ordinary people. She is skilled in immersing the linguistic fundamentals in icy humor, fluid colors, authentic and inauthentic voices, fleeting consciousness and non-ultimate philosophy.

In colloquial expression, her characters are ordinary and yet extraordinary. Her language has color, sound, and smell. Her writings provide both strong pictorial and audio images, which invite the reader to enter easily into the scenes and situations that she created.